A HERO FOR THE PEOPLE

A HERO FOR THE PEOPLE
Stories of the Brazilian Backlands

ARTHUR POWERS

Press 53
Winston-Salem

Press 53, LLC
PO Box 30314
Winston-Salem, NC 27130

First Edition

Cover design by Kevin Morgan Watson

Cover photograph, "Montanhas Azuis–Blue Mountains"
Copyright © 2013 by Augusto Froehlich,
used by permission.

Author photo by Caroline Powers

This is a work of fiction. Names, characters, places, and incidents
are products of the author's imagination or are used fictionally.
Any resemblance to actual events, locales, or persons,
living or dead, is entirely coincidental.

Printed on acid-free paper
ISBN 978-1-935708-83-4

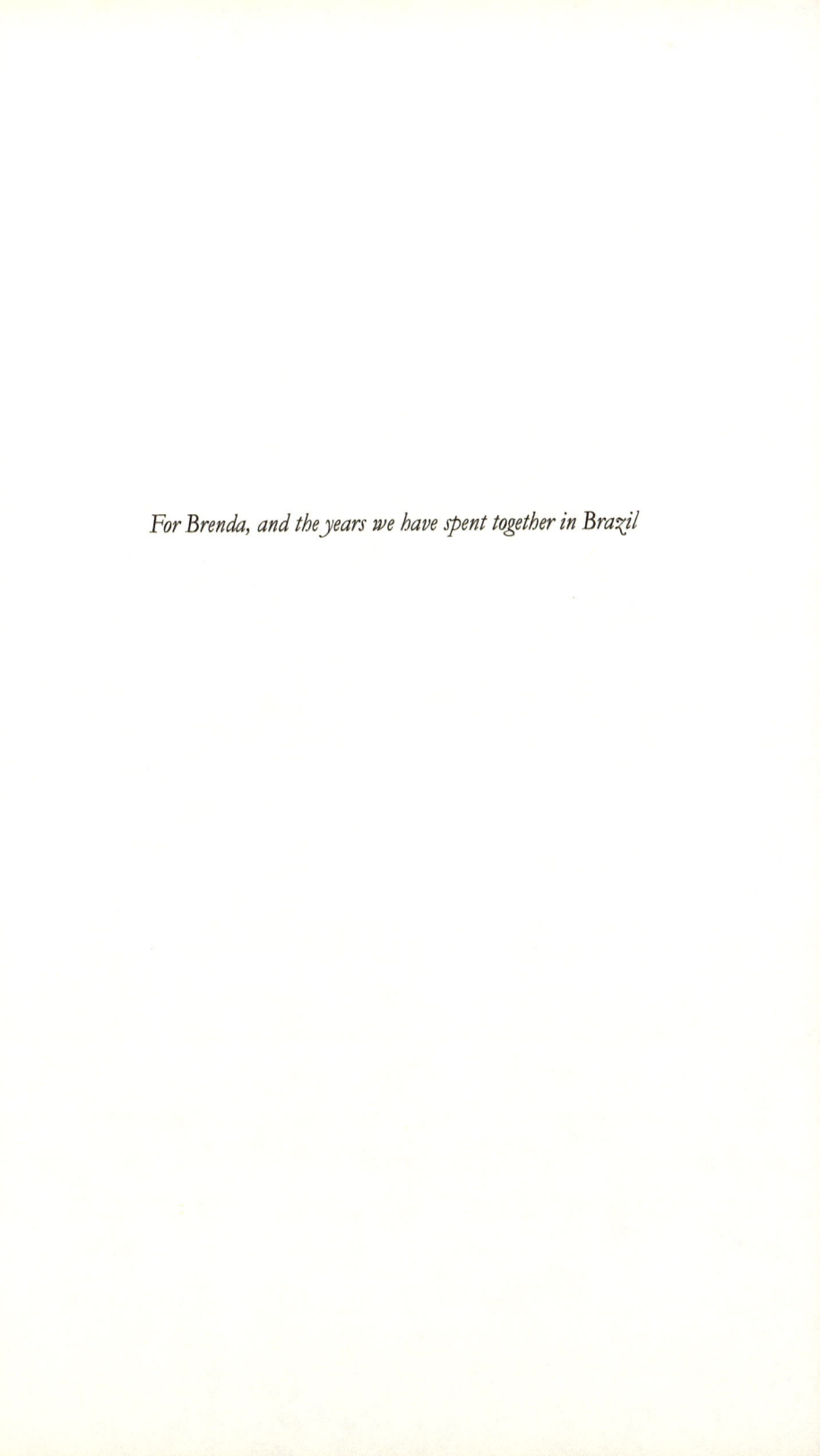

For Brenda, and the years we have spent together in Brazil

ACKNOWLEDGMENTS

The author received a Fellowship in Fiction from the Massachusetts Artists Foundation (1984) based on three of the stories in this volume: "Gilsa," "The Moving," and "Come Into My House And Stay." "Gilsa" was also highly commended in the 2008 Tom Howard Short Story Contest.

"Cláudio" appeared in *Critic*.

"A Hero For The People," "Stone," "Carla," and "Come Into My House And Stay" appeared in *Dappled Things*. "Carla" was nominated for a 2012 Pushcart Prize.

"The Healer" appeared in *Liguorian* under the title, "Pastor Eugênio's Confession." It was awarded 3rd place for short fiction by the Catholic Press Association (2006). "Colors" (under the title "God's Color Wheel") also appeared in *Liguorian*.

"The Bridge," "Back Country People," and "Switzerland" appeared in *St. Anthony Messenger*. "The Bridge" was awarded 1st place (1995) and "Back Country People" 2nd place (1998) for short fiction by the Catholic Press Association. "The Bridge" also received 2nd place in the 2008 Tom Howard Short Story Contest and was a Finalist in the 2012 Press 53 Open Awards. "Back Country People" was a Finalist in the 2011 Press 53 Open Awards.

"Hate" appeared in *The Worcester Review*.

"Famine" and "Two Foxes" appeared in *XNK Magazine*. "Famine" was a Finalist in the 2012 Press 53 Open Awards.

"Two Foxes" and "Four Liters of Wild Honey" appeared in the anthology: *Being Human: Call of the Wild* (Editions Bibliotekos, 2012).

A Hero for the People
Stories of the Brazilian Backlands

Note on the Text

Brazil is an enormous and highly diverse country. These stories are set in various regions: the savannah lands of the Central West & eastern Amazon, the rain forest, the semi-arid Northeast, the cities of Rio de Janeiro and Recife. Each story has a geographic location and a date—this is the date in which the events occur, not the year in which the story was written.

The author first went to Brazil with the Peace Corps in 1969 and spent most his adult life there. He has lived in the locations in which the stories are set (Espírito Santo, Bahia, Rio de Janeiro, Tocantins/Northern Goiás[1], Recife) and worked with people very much like the people in these stories.

Certain historical factors are important to the background of these stories. From 1964 to 1985, Brazil was governed by a military dictatorship. Beginning in the 1970s, violent land conflicts broke out in the Brazilian Central West and eastern Amazon (such conflicts have been common throughout Brazilian history), especially in the states of Pará, Mato Grosso, and Tocantins. Among the many people killed were Fr. Josimo Tavares, a Catholic priest, in 1987, and Sister Dorothy Stang in 2005. The author and his wife lived in that region from 1985 to 1992, organizing subsistence farmers and rural workers' unions.

---

[1] The present State of Tocantins was created in 1988. It was previously the northern half of the State of Goiás.

THE BRIDGE
(Northern Goiás, 1987)

1

Nobody dreams as a kid that they're going to grow up and live in the Central West of Brazil. Rio de Janeiro, maybe, or the rainforests of the Amazon. But not the hot, flat grasslands that stretch between the Tocantins and Araguaia Rivers, lands of huge cattle ranches, half-hungry dirt farmers, and dusty, dirty little towns. Then one morning you're about forty-five years old and standing out in the vegetable garden behind one of the decaying white parish houses in one of those dusty towns, and it occurs to you that you've spent the best part of your adult life out here and, in all likelihood, will spend the rest of it here too. That's obvious, of course, and you've known it all along—but suddenly, standing there in the garden, it hits you like a two-ton truck. So you either say a prayer, laugh, and get back to work—or you go crazy.

Not that we're not all a little crazy anyway. You get that way after a while, and it comes out in crazy little ways: a twitching of the left eye, a conviction that somebody's stealing spoons from the kitchen, an obsession with baseball scores heard over the Voice of America. Harmless insanities that allow men to function normally—even magnificently—in the middle of nowhere, year after year after year.

At first I thought Jack Hogan had something like that. I'd taken a few days off and was visiting him down at the mission in Santa Maria das Dores—one of our dusty little towns. Jack and I had been classmates at the seminary, friends from way back. He had a couple of young Brazilian priests working with him—good men, both of them—and the four of us were sitting around the rectory, sharing a bottle of beer and having fun talking about nothing in particular, when a message came that the bishop wanted to talk to Jack on the phone. The only phone in town was at the telephone office down on the main street. So Jack and I walked down there.

There are times like that—coming out of the good fellowship in the parish house—that those towns really hit you—slap you across the face with their ugliness, their pain and poverty and injustice—so little beauty or caring or love. That's why we're here, of course; that's why we stay. But it hits you anyway, knocks the breath out of you: the hopelessness of the place, the guilt you feel at your own privilege—being able to eat three meals a day—and the whole damn unfairness of it: a handful of rich men running one of the richest countries in the world for their own benefit, while two thirds of the people go hungry.

That afternoon, as we walked out, there was a thin, weedy black woman hugging a baby to her. I didn't know her—Santa Maria is one of the few towns of ours I've never worked in, which is maybe why I like to visit there: don't know the people and the stories that haunt and twist their lives. Anyway, Jack stopped to talk to her. We spent about fifteen minutes—you know how country people are: you could tell she wanted to say something, but she talked about everything else first, until it finally came out that her husband had taken off the week before and she had no food for her kids. So we spent a few more minutes; Jack cared about her—you could see that, *she* could see that—and part of caring is that you try not to just give people hand-outs—it can cripple them more—but try to help them help each other. But, of course, none of it's simple—you have to know each person, and what will help them and what won't, and you make mistakes all the time. In the end she walked with us a little way to where Jack took her into the house of a couple who are organizing a church food cooperative.

I waited for Jack outside. As I was waiting, an old man I knew came up to me—Seu Zé Touro. He was a dirt farmer from Barro Branco, about a hundred miles north of Santa Maria, and I'd worked closely with him and his neighbors, helping them organize to stay on the land when a big rancher wanted them off. They'd struggled and they'd stayed. But recently I'd heard that his nephew had been killed by another landowner's gunmen in another area. I didn't know what to say to him—he was close to the nephew, had raised him from a boy—but I told him that I'd heard and that I was sorry.

He looked at me. He was a thin, blond man with a craggy, sunburned face and pale, watery eyes. Nothing about him—just looking at him, I mean—showed you how tough he was, but I knew him and he was steel-strong inside, able to hold out day after day, year after year, under all kinds of pressure. But he was a quiet, gentle man, and he looked down at the ground, then up again before saying anything.

"Padre, I figure that when a person's hour comes, it comes, and there isn't much we can do about it, one way or another. Wherever he is, it'll happen."

It wasn't a new thought—I'd heard it a hundred times before from the people. My North American mind always rebels against it, and I don't know what I think of it theologically, but if it helps these people face life and death, and maybe stand up and fight for their land…? Who knows, maybe they're right. Maybe the only freedom we have isn't when we die, but how—if it's not a bullet while resisting a rich landowner, it could be a truck hitting us on the streets of New York or São Paulo, or a heart attack in our back yard. Maybe our only choice in the matter is whether we die with courage or like cowards or like some nothing in between. How the hell should I know?

About then, Jack came out of the house. We shook hands with Seu Zé and started along the street. The sun was intensely hot—making the street a kind of blank, blinding hell: you could almost hear the heat singing off the plastered walls, smell it rising out of the dust. The futility of it all hit me again—how for every woman you help find food, every farmer you help stay on the land, there are a hundred, two hundred, five hundred more you can never help.

All the way to the telephone office, of course, it was the same—people stopping Jack with things they wanted: an old man demanding that Jack baptize his grandson next Saturday, a small farmer asking for help with his land title, a woman angrily wanting to know why the mayor had given her neighbor a free blanket and not given her one—something Jack had nothing to do with. It took another half hour to walk four blocks—it's always like that when you walk through the town where you're stationed. That's why some of the guys always go by jeep, even for a few blocks. Of course there are other ways: Frank Davis rides a bicycle—says it allows him to get by with a wave and a friendly word, and whiz off before anyone corners him; Billy Martin has been pretending for years that he's half deaf.

In any case, we got to the telephone office and waited another forty minutes for the call to go through—there's only one line into town—and the operator telling Jack about her problems with her husband. When we got through the bishop wasn't there, but Brother Pedro was, and he said that the bishop asked if Jack could go up to Miracema the next day and talk to the bishop. Jack wasn't real pleased about it, but he said he would and I told him I'd go along for the ride.

2

It was on the way up that it first happened. Not that I thought much about it then.

We had driven the jeep ninety kilometers over the dirt road to the Belém-Brasília, the only paved highway linking southern Brazil to the north. Recently it's started breaking into pot holes and sinking back into the earth, but at that time it was still a good road: two lanes, smoothly paved with clear markings and reasonably wide shoulders. It looked just like a small American highway and you could pretend you were riding along through Iowa or Nebraska, except when a small mountain made you think of Pennsylvania, or a jagged butte—a monster rising out of nowhere—took you to Wyoming or Montana.

It was like an American highway except for the bridges. There are maybe twenty or thirty of them along the stretch we were traveling—not big bridges, but the kind that cross creeks and small streams. You don't even notice them, really: the road stays flat and you wouldn't see the bridges if it weren't for the cement railings and the signs. Oh, yes—they have signs, even in Brazil, marking the names of the creeks you're passing over:

big green road signs, easily visible even at night, just like in the United States. They may not have hospitals or schools or food for the people, but they have beautiful big road signs giving information nobody needs or wants. They wouldn't want you to think they were a backward nation.

The cement railings are another matter. Square cement posts whited like tombstones stand frighteningly close to the road, leaving very little shoulder, thin cement railings running between them. There's really plenty of room, of course, but when you're headed onto one of those bridges with, say, a giant Scania truck roaring down at you from the other side, you're kind of inclined to miss a heart beat, hold your breath, and hope like hell you'll get through. You always do—at least I always have. Then again, on about half the bridges part of the railings are smashed out where somebody hit them and, maybe, went over.

Anyhow, we were approaching one of the bridges—the big green sign read "Córrego Vermelho"—when I noticed that Jack slowed down the jeep a bit and then accelerated, as if suddenly in a hurry. We were alone on the highway—nothing coming the other way—so I didn't think much of it until we were on the bridge and I glanced at Jack.

He was shuddering and deathly pale; beads of sweat stood on his forehead and his fingers clutched the wheel so hard his knuckles were white. He was watching the road intently, as though he had to guide the jeep through some deadly, narrow spot, so I waited until we were off the bridge before I spoke.

"You okay?" I asked.

He didn't answer for a moment. When he did, it was with a deep, scratchy voice, as though he had to drag the words out of his throat.

"Sure," he said.

We rode for another kilometer or so before I said, "It's the bridge, isn't it? I know—I have the same feeling. You get onto one of those bridges and you start to imagine what it would be like to smash into one side or the other—how easy it would be to do it—the crashing sound of metal, the shock of impact, the cement posts breaking, the jeep going over the edge..."

I turned toward him and was startled to find he was looking at me—looking at me with wide eyes, a strange naked expression on his face as though I'd uncovered some dark hidden sin. I suppose it was only a moment's glance, but it seemed like minutes that he sat there, his eyes on me as we sped along the highway. I broke my eyes away and looked out the windshield.

"Watch out!" I shouted, and he recovered and swerved around a Mercedes truck that had pulled out ahead of us onto the road.

There were plenty of other bridges on the way, but we passed over them without even noticing. By the time we reached Miracema, the incident was behind us—we hadn't mentioned it, and were talking and laughing like our normal selves.

The meeting with the bishop was important. I don't know what sixth sense it is you get down here—maybe it's the Holy Spirit guiding you; God knows, by all earthly standards the Church and the poor it works for should have been defeated years ago. But sometimes these warnings come, and the bishop had woken up the morning before with the feeling that another spurt of violence by landowners was going to start. So he called together eighteen or twenty of the people most active in land issues—a handful of priests, five or six sisters, the lawyer for the land commission, several union leaders. In the end, that meeting saved a lot of small landholdings and probably several lives. But Jack wasn't really part of it by then.

Next day after lunch we started back toward Santa Maria. About mid-afternoon I was lost in thought, looking out the window, when the jeep started to slow and Jack brought it to a halt on the shoulder. I looked at him. He was pale and sweating—it flashed across my mind that he might have malaria—his hands clenched the wheel, the motor still running with the hard thumping heartbeat of an idling jeep.

"What's wrong?" I asked.

He didn't answer but nodded his head forward. I looked and saw, about a hundred yards ahead, the sign: "Córrego Vermelho."

I recognized the place, but I was absolutely baffled.

"What is it?" I asked.

He shook his head.

"I don't know," he said, almost whispering. He had calmed down some now and started the car forward again, but as soon as he did so he began to sweat and shake, breathing with short urgent panting. He pulled to a stop again. A car swept by us, tooting its horn.

"You want me to drive?"

He nodded, switched off the motor, and slumped back in his seat. I got out, walked around the jeep and, opening his door, put my hand on his shoulder.

"Come on," I said.

He turned and slid down from his seat until he was standing on the ground. He was looking down at his feet.

"Sorry," he said. "I don't know…"

His voice trailed off. His breathing was regular now, but he was still sweating.

That's okay," I said. "We all push ourselves too hard

sometimes," —which, God knows, is true enough. "Get in. I'll drive back."

It took a few minutes. He stood still, husbanding his strength, then started lumbering around the front of the jeep, holding onto it, as though for support. His movements were, I knew, a pure act of will. I waited; I didn't want to hurry him and it wasn't right to help him: sometimes there are things a man has to do on his own.

Finally he got in on the other side, sitting hard on the seat, leaning back and closing his eyes.

"Okay?" I asked.

"Go ahead," he answered after a moment. I sensed again that he had to drag the words from somewhere deep down inside.

I started the jeep, waited for a couple of trucks to pass, then pulled out slowly toward the bridge. We were about thirty feet from it, moving slowly, when Jack suddenly shot upright in the seat beside me.

"Stop!" he yelled in pure terror. He opened the door and bolted out. I slammed on the brake and pulled over, killed the motor and jumped out of the jeep.

Jack was standing by the road and I ran back toward him. As I got close I realized he was in a panic. He was shivering and sweating, and his eyes, big and almost glazed, were fastened on the bridge.

"Hey, Jack," I said gently. "What is it?"

He seemed to hear me, but it took a few seconds for him to answer.

"The bridge," he said at last.

"What about the bridge?" I looked over at it, putting an arm around his shoulders. "Is it going to fall?" How did I know? Maybe it was his sixth sense warning us of danger. But he shook his head.

"Let's walk over and take a look at it," I said. I was praying silently: "Dear God, let me know what to do."

You can't be in our work as long as I have without seeing people break, but it still doesn't help you know what to do: each person is different. Just be gentle and firm, pray a lot, and listen.

We walked slowly over to the bridge and I reached out and touched the first cement post. They're about three feet high, maybe a foot and a half wide on each side, square—but slightly rounded at the top, painted white. I thought again of tombstones. After a moment Jack reached out and touched it too, like a school kid touching a strange animal—fascinated yet afraid, as though the post might bite. He held his hand there for half a minute, stroking the cement, then drew it back.

"Do you want to walk across, and I'll bring the car?"

He looked at the bridge. "No."

I glanced around me and thought. We could have turned back to Miracema, but that seemed pointless. I wanted to get Jack home to Santa Maria, but he wouldn't drive across the bridge, and he wouldn't walk across.

There was another way—there always is. I looked toward the creek. The land sloped down to it about thirty feet on this side, then up on the other. It was fairly steep and covered with thick grass, but we could make it. The creek itself was only about ten feet across, probably two or three deep.

"Would the creek bother you?" I asked.

He looked at me blankly.

"Could you wade across the creek?"

He looked down at it. "Sure."

"Then let's go."

I started down the slope, half sliding, half walking, hoping there wouldn't be any snakes in the under-growth. After a moment I heard him climbing down behind me. I reached the bank and began to stamp down the grass around a boulder that was there, making a place to sit down. Jack finished clambering down and I sat down and started to take of my shoes and socks. "Take off your shoes," I said. He stared for a moment, then sat down. He had sandals on and he unbuckled them, painfully, slowly, but he was doing it and I knew again that every movement was an act of will, demanding tremendous effort and courage.

He paused and looked out at the water, then spoke, the words again dragged up from deep underneath — deep underneath layers of mind and nerves that told him what he said or did was meaningless, didn't matter, made no difference.

"You don't have to wade across," he said.

The bravery of it made me stop in awe. I smiled at him, wanting to show I appreciated it.

"Hey," I said. "We're in this together." He was still staring at the water. "Besides," I said, "I could stand to be rebaptized."

He actually smiled at that — a thin smile, but then it was pretty thin humor. I picked up my shoes and socks and started across the stream, shuffling my feet in case there were sting rays along the muddy bottom. He followed me, holding his sandals high and balancing against the small current as though he were a tight-rope walker. It was deeper than I'd thought — four, almost four and a half feet in the middle — but we made it through. There were some flat rocks on the other side and we sat on them, letting the sun dry us a little, looking at the stream.

"Well, we did it," I said lightly.

"Yes," he answered, and I suddenly knew that what, for me, had been a short climb and wade, had been for him a journey — a day's trek, maybe — or a lifetime's. He was staring out over the stream with a look on his face, in his eyes, that a mountain climber might wear when he was resting at the summit of a difficult climb.

"Do you think we could head back up to the road?"
I asked. It was like asking the mountain climber if we
could go back down the mountain: of course we could.
I pulled on my socks and shoes; he buckled his sandals—
slowly, determinedly. Then we turned and started up,
side by side.

Jack was exhausted by the time we reached the
highway—pale and drained, but not shaking.
"Why don't you sit and rest for a couple of minutes
and I'll go get the jeep." It was easy enough; I would
just have to walk back across the bridge.
He sat down on the gravel beside the road, and I was
just about to start back when I heard him sob. I squatted
down beside him.
"I'm sorry," he sobbed. "I'm sorry."
I put an arm around his shoulders and just let him
cry and cry and cry.

3

Everyone was very understanding. They flew Jack back
to the States, where he went to one of those places for
people who work too hard and care too much, where
you can rest and pray and there's someone who will
listen. I got two or three letters from him while he was
there. I remember that in one of them he wrote, "I feel
like I've faced fear and won."
When he recuperated he was sent out to work in a
parish in the Western states. He was very happy there,
and apparently made quite an impact. Once when I was
in New York I met a young woman from Jack's parish.
She was attractive, clean-cut and strong-limbed; she later
entered a missionary order of sisters. As we were talking
about Jack, she said, "He was so fearless about looking
straight into things—into life…" She was groping for

words, and I think she felt she hadn't articulated very well. But I knew what she meant.

Jack didn't write often once he got back to work. When you're in a parish, you think a lot about writing but almost never have time to do so. I did get one letter from him, though. He told all the news about his work, mutual friends, life in the States. He went on to write:

"Whatever it was on that bridge, it wasn't just nerves. Oh, I know it was the nerves—the stress, the exhaustion—that made me panic, that made me go to pieces. But there was something there, something dangerous. Whatever it is—*wherever* it is (I don't think it's in Brazil anymore), I'll meet it again sometime. But this time I'll meet it with courage."

Six months later we received a telegram. Jack had been killed in Idaho when his car crashed crossing the Vermillion Creek bridge.

BACK COUNTRY PEOPLE
(Tocantins, 1992)

I t was late afternoon when Zé Dias stepped out of Manoel Vermelho's little dirt-floored bar into the rich glowing sunlight, and there wasn't a sign of life out there except for a plume of smoke rising from Manoel's house down the way and a yellow-brown dog asleep in the middle of the yellow-brown dirt crossroads. Trees and grass and Manoel's scraggly cornfield behind a barbed wire fence, but no people. Most important, no sign of the kid.

"Maybe he's wandered off," Zé Dias hoped as he started for his pick-up, for if the kid wasn't there Zé Dias would be off the hook and could drive right back to Itacajá, which was where he wanted to be. But just then he saw the kid stand up lean and lanky from the running board where he'd been sitting on the shady side of the clay colored Toyota pick-up, and turn toward Zé Dias with wide simple eyes that tugged Zé Dias' conscience.

Back country people. Always wanting something, always looking at you in that dumb, innocent way so that you couldn't say no. Sure, they helped each other all the time, but then how often did they see anyone except their own family — once every few days, once a week? You could afford to help everyone that way, but in town, he, Zé Dias, saw what — a couple of hundred, five hundred, maybe a thousand people a day? And could he stop and help every one of them the way back country people did? Of course not: any idiot could see that. And yet here was this kid, looking at him and reminding him of his promise.

The boy had come into Manoel's bar shortly after Zé Dias arrived. The bar served as a small general store, and Zé Dias had goods to deliver — cartons of flashlight batteries, cigarettes, match boxes, cases of *cachaça*, gallons of kerosene, *fardas* of salt. Invoices to be checked, payments to be received, credits to be worked out. Manoel was there, and a couple of men and an old woman, *curiando*, as the people said, wanting to know everything that was going on. And the kid standing by the door — and Zé Dias, sitting on a stool at the bar going over invoices, knowing the kid wanted something and trying to ignore him.

Manoel looked up and saw the kid. "What can we do for you?" Manoel said, the shop-keeper coming out strong in him like an instinct.

"My father," the boy said, looking at Manoel and talking in that dignified way back country people sometimes had, as though every word had been planned out a long time ago. "He has malaria. He's dying. We need to take him to Pedro Afonso."

Zé Dias sat on his stool intensely examining lists of figures as though what the boy said had nothing to do with him, as though he didn't know his pick-up was the only vehicle within fifty kilometers. Pretend dumb. If they have to ask you, sometimes they don't. Then you have no responsibility.

"About this invoice..." he started to say, glancing up.

Manoel was looking at him. The old woman was looking at him. The two men were looking at him. The boy was looking at him.

"This invoice..." he started again, but it was no use; his words stumbled on their silence. They were expecting something of him. Back country people, every one of them—even Manoel Vermelho who ran the store and gouged his neighbors for all Zé Dias knew. They wanted him to go get this sick man; all of them, who'd never driven a car, much less owned one, standing there wanting Zé Dias to do something they'd never be called on to do. Back country people, always expecting something.

"What's the problem?" Zé Dias asked, playing stupid, and the eyes switched collectively to the kid, who shuffled and looked embarrassed. He's not really a boy, Zé Dia noticed—twenty or twenty-two years old, but with that sunburned country innocence that made you think he was younger. And thin—the kid was thin. This had been a bad year in the back country.

"My father. He has malaria," the boy repeated, as though he were reciting a script, but this time looking at Zé Dias. "We need to take him to Pedro Afonso."

"I'm not going to Pedro Afonso," Zé Dias said, "just to Itacajá." But even he knew he was stalling.

"If you would take us to where the road divides..." Zé Dias knew the rest: they could get the bus from there to Pedro Afonso in the morning.

"Who's your father?" he asked. It was almost a tacit acceptance of responsibility.

"Inácio Mário Ferreira dos Santos." The boy quoted his father's name in the rote way back country people always did, which was never any help because no one used their full names.

"Inácio de Tiago," one of the men said helpfully, using the man's nickname.

"You know him," the old woman said. "His niece, Marli, is married to Mariano Pinto's son in Itacajá." And Zé Dias remembered a man named Inácio sitting on one of the rawhide stools in front of Mariano Pinto's store.

"A big man," Zé Dias said. He reached his hand up and touched his hair: "With a balding head."

"That's him," the old woman said.

Not a man Zé Dias liked. A pompous, self-important dirt farmer, always talking about the Bible. But he had no choice.

"How far is it?" he asked the kid.

"Not far."

Back country people!—not far—nothing was ever far when they wanted you to go there.

"What does that mean?" he asked, intentionally exaggerating, "five *léguas*, six?" He looked at Manoel Vermelho.

"About two," Manoel shrugged. Which meant two-and-a-half or three. Fifteen to eighteen kilometers; double to get there and back.

"What's the road like?" Zé Dias asked. It was his final surrender.

"It's a good road," the kid said. Which, Zé Dias knew, meant absolutely nothing.

Between 5:55 and 6:30 p.m., it switches from afternoon to complete dark, and it was dark when they hit the turn-off, Zé Dias driving, the kid at the passenger window, his arm latched out into the night air. The turn-off was a white strip of sand set in the brush.

"That's the road?" Zé Dias exclaimed, but it really wasn't as bad as he'd expected. As he turned, he could see it in the headlights stretching straight white ahead of them. Then, thirty meters down the road, the kid said, "Turn in here."

Ze Dias stopped the pick-up. "There's no road," he said, but the kid pointed with his arm and Zé Dias saw two dim wheel tracks heading off to the left.

"You sure we can pass there?" Zé Dias asked.

The kid nodded. "This is the way cars come."

Back country people. This is the way cars come, as though the kid knew anything about cars. Zé Dias shifted into first and turned onto the track. There were a couple of small bumps and the pick-up lilted along, its headlights shining directly into the tall palm grass growing between the ruts as high as the hood. The track began to curve to the right, but it was smooth, and the pick-up made a soft swishing sound as it pushed down the grass in front of it—a boat sailing through a grass sea. Sailing quickly—at this rate they'd get there and back in good time.

Bump, jolt: the steering wheel nearly knocked out of his hands, the sound of the pick-up's suspension hitting bottom—whack! for the front wheels, whack! again for the back, the pick-up moving along the track, Zé Dias slowing down.

"A little gully where the rain water washed the dirt out," the kid said.

"I noticed," Zé Dias felt like saying, but his mouth was clamped shut. It took him a minute to pry it open. "When was this road last fixed up?" he asked.

"It was grated during the last election," the kid said.

"That was over a year ago," Zé Dias said. "How long has it been since a truck came through here?"

"The last election," the kid said.

Zé Dias slammed on the brake and the pick-up skidded into another series of bumps. He winced, feeling the pain of the suspension and axels and tires as if they were part of his body.

"I've got to be crazy to drive the pick-up down this road," he said, but he said it into silence, the kid just sitting there in the night, sitting in the passenger's seat, calm and inevitable as conscience, his arm latched out the window.

They moved slowly along the track. It came out of the high grasses and onto open savannah, the light beams picking out the traces of road a hundred feet ahead of them. Night bugs batted against the windshield and three or four times the lights picked out ground owls, looking like brown rocks except for the glassy red glint of their eyes reflecting the headlights. The owls would sit in the road unmovable until just before the car was on them, then would take off and away at a steep angle. The scrub brush reached out from the sides of the road, scraping along the clay colored sides of the Toyota.

Zé Dias drove with half his mind carefully negotiating the track, wincing at the bumps and scratches and strange muffled sounds of plants tangling the bottom of the pick-up. The other half of his mind was picturing his house in Itacajá—his comfortable bed—wishing he were in it, fighting off sleep as the road went on for what seemed hours and hours. One could think one had died and was on the road to heaven and would be on it forever, jostled along over dirt and sand and stone. The road passed through a jungle area, and vines caught at the side mirrors, the vines dry and snapping broken as the pick-up pulled them taut. Savannah again, and the lights shining ahead, the angle of their beam making little mounds appear to be deep holes, slowing him down almost to a stop when there was nothing there to really bother about. Or, at times, not looking like anything much, and the pick-up moving too quickly into a bone-breaking jolt.

The pick-up came to a halt, its motor thump-thumping against the chirping and cheeing of the jungle night. The track had disappeared on a slope—higher on the left, lower on the right—where the rains had eroded away any trace of ruts, leaving huge gravelly wrinkles of red-tan earth.

"We can't get through that," Zé Dias said, and the kid didn't say anything. Back country people. A townsperson would have argued, would have bargained, would have said, "My father is dying," but back country people lived in a slower, deeper place. Something said was said, it did not have to be said again. His father was dying, but deep down Zé Dias knew, and thought that the boy knew, that wasn't the question. The journey, the getting there, were Zé Dias' now—he owned them, would fight for them, would accomplish them. He would complain, curse the wear on his pick-up, and hope for some obstacle big enough to stop him and make him turn around, but he would go on.

Reaching down and shifting into four-wheel drive, he moved the pick-up slowly forward, angling the wheels over the bumps and gullies so that the front end wouldn't dive down and catch in the dirt. He was sweating now, even with the windows open against the cool jungle night. Twenty meters of it and they were through, the grass growing tall in front of them and no sign whatsoever of the track.

"Where's the road?" Zé Dias asked, and the kid leaned forward, gesturing his hand and arm in a slow semi-circular motion at the grass in front of them. "It's all clear through there, you can drive anywhere," the kid said.

Drive anywhere! Back country people. They were always thinking cars were like horses. They would clear roadways and leave *tocos*, little stumps of hatcheted saplings, barely an inch or so from the ground, no problem for horses or buggies or bicycles or men on foot, but disaster to tires weighed down with a half a ton of metal.

"Do you know what you're talking about?" Zé Dias said. "Last month Padre Jaime was on a road like this out near Colher and he got two flat tires—not one, but two. Had to wait three days until they could get new tires out to him. Do you know how much tires cost?" But even as he spoke he was inching the pick-up through the tall grass, feeling the green entangling plants grabbing at the axles of the car as though they were grabbing his legs.

"More to the left," the kid said. He was leaning forward, his face close to the windshield, his eyes straining into the dark, where the headlights lit up almost nothing except the tall pale green grass that rose like a curtain in front of them.

We'll pay for your fuel, back country people were always saying, trying to get drivers to go out of their way, to carry a hog or a barrel of flour or an old grandmother four kilometers down a side road. As if a few litres of diesel made the difference, as if tires and suspension and axles weren't worth a hundred times the cost of fuel. What did they know, these back country people, who'd never had to buy parts for a pick-up? He'd charge them more than fuel, for sure, but it wasn't worth the wear on the truck, the lost time.

"That way, further," the kid said, motioning with his hand over to the left, and then the grass stopped and they were at the edge of a dip—white clay going down three or four meters at a forty-five degree angle to a small stream, then angling up on the other side. Zé Dias stopped the pick-up, turned off the motor, opened the door and stood up on the running board, his body braced against the open door, looking down the slope, judging the depth of the stream, the wetness and hardness of the white clay.

The night was dark, the sky bright with stars but with no moon. The grass was alive with the chirping of insects and somewhere downstream frogs were singing in rubbery, grating voices. Off to the left was the shadowed outline of tall trees, and Zé Dias heard the chee of a monkey.

He smiled a half-smile, loving night sounds, before pulling himself back into the truck and sitting down.

"That's a ford?" he asked the kid, and the kid nodded.

"There hasn't been much rain," the kid said, which was true enough, the rice crop dried up on most of these back country farms, the corn struggling. Good thing, too, tonight—in the rainy season, his pick-up would have slithered down that clay, hub deep in mud, stuck at the bottom, and never climbed up the other side.

"If we stick, kid, this trip's finished," Zé Dias, said. And it'll be *my* problem, not theirs, he thought, getting a pick-up out of a silly damned gulch in the middle of nowhere. He turned on the motor, checked the four wheel drive, shifted into first, and started down the slope.

The adobe farmhouse's wooden door was open, letting the light from the kerosene lantern flow out into the night. They had probably heard the motor coming for the last half hour, Zé Dias thought as he pulled the pick-up to a stop. The silence with the engine off—night sounds around—was beautiful and peaceful. Zé Dias heard the pick-up's door slam behind him, clear and satisfying in the night, granting a brief rest for a job half done.

Through the door, Zé Dias could see the stark light of the kerosene lantern unnaturally bright on the bare white walls. Four sixty-kilo sacks of rice lay stacked against the wall, and a fifth stood beside the doorway, a pitiful harvest for a back country family. A corn husk mattress, covered in blue cloth with wild orange flowers on printed vines, lay on top of clean woven straw mats that were spread on the dirt floor. A small, pale woman, about forty, with dark hair knotted back on her head, had just helped a tall man to stand up; a boy of about eighteen was supporting the man from the other side. It took Zé Dias a minute to realize that the tall man was Inácio—the large, strong-willed man who spoke in a deep voice while his finger moved up and down, citing lessons from the Bible, now looked fragile and thin, trembling and yellow, held up by a woman and a boy.

"Get the mattress," the woman said to the kid who had come with Zé Dias, and the kid ran in and picked up the mattress, bringing it out to the canvas-covered back of the pick-up. He unlatched the back and got up into the bed of the truck, laying out the mattress, then helping his brother lift their father onto the mattress, laying him down. Zé Dias went over to help them, taking hold of one of Inácio's legs, but they really didn't need his help. Their father settled, the younger brother went back to the door, picked up the sack of rice, hoisted it over his shoulder, and brought it back to the truck. It would fetch a little money at the mill in Pedro Afonso—not much, Zé Dias knew, but it was what they could spare.

"We can go now," the older kid said, and Zé Dias realized how worried they were. Usually at back country houses they went all out for any visitor, and especially a visitor doing a favor: conversation, a small cup of thick, sugary coffee or—in these days when people were too poor to have coffee—a glass of water, a sweet home-made tea. A share in the meal if there was one, a hunk of sugar cane, a piece of fruit. Never a hurry.

But there was urgency here. He turned back to the truck, thinking how much he would have liked some coffee. He glanced at his watch and discovered it was only nine-thirty. It felt like midnight.

He climbed in the cab of the pick-up. The younger brother was riding with him now, the elder in back with his father. Zé Dias started the motor and the sound roared into the jungle night. He started to back up the truck, but the woman was at the window, pale, her dark eyes worried.

The woman, who probably would, but might never, see her husband again.

"We thank you," she said.

The road back wasn't any better than the road out. They were three hours to Manoel Vermelho's house and bar at the crossroads, the darkened adobe buildings passing quickly, shadows against the night. Then another three hours to Santa Maria, the village where the road split— one branch going to Pedro Afonso, the other to Itacajá. So there was a faint paling of the sky in the east as they unloaded the sick man, the mattress, and the rice onto the thatch covered porch from where the bus would leave in a couple of hours. The village was quiet, and Zé Dias could hear the sounds of the brothers settling their father on the wooden porch, and his own footsteps on the dirt and gravel street as he walked back toward the pick-up.

He was in it and had the motor started when the kid— the first kid, the older kid—was at the window.

"How much do we owe you?" the kid asked.

"That's okay," Zé Dias heard himself saying. "You don't owe me anything."

The kid was quiet for a moment.

"Thanks," he said.

Zé Dias nodded. He lightly gunned the pick-up. The kid stood away from the window and Zé Dias started up, turning sharp right onto the Itacajá road—two hours of narrow, bumpy, but harmless gravel road would see him home. Back country people, he thought, they're always getting something out of you. The sky was a little less dark and, outside in the trees, the birds were starting to get noisy, and Zé Dias was tired, good tired, up-driving-all-night tired. The pick-up headed smoothly if a little bumpily toward home, and Zé Dias started quietly singing.

HATE
(Massachusetts and Northern Goiás, 1989)

We make a point of getting together as often as we can, especially every few years when Dave Sorensen is home from Brazil. The four of us have one of those friendships that picks up where it left off, no matter how long it's been since we've seen one another. It's as though twenty-five years drop away and we're sitting around Elliot House in one of our all-night bull sessions, though of course we know a lot more—and *think* we know a lot less—than we did then. We laugh a lot, propound crazy theories, jibe at one another. But somehow we cut through the superficiality that most of us mouth most of the time, and talk about things that matter, muddling along to see if we can find out what life is all about. Which, I suppose, *is* what life is all about.

That night we were at Bob Crawford's house in Needham. Connie and Marge Crawford had taken Ann Sorensen to a concert, and Paul's wife was visiting her folks in Connecticut, so there were just the four of us, sitting in the family room, drinking beer. Bob's big balding head glistened in the light of the floor lamp. Everything about Bob is big: his smile, his laugh, the checks on his sports shirts, his hefty ex-footballer's frame. He looks exactly like what he is—a sports writer for the *Globe*. Paul, on the other hand, his hair prematurely (I like to think) gray, always looks distinguished, even with his jacket off, his tie undone, and a glass of beer in his hand.

But it was Dave, with his jungle-tanned face and trim black beard, who usually was the fittest of any of us, despite the hardship of his life—or maybe because of it. Yet, during his home leave this year, we had noticed a tired, haunted look in Dave's eyes, a certain restlessness in his manner. Connie once said that Dave reminded her of Moses' fiery bush—always burning but never consumed. It seemed this summer that the flames had eaten away at him a little. Of course we knew the pressures he and Ann were under—the land struggles, the threats to their lives. Still, that had been going on for years.

I don't know how we got to talking about ghosts. We wandered into the subject, half-remembering stories we'd half-heard from doubtful sources. Finally Bob said:

"It all depends on the purity of your heart."

"What do you mean?" I asked.

"Well, take a lonely cemetery at night." Bob lowered his voice for effect. "Pale moonlight, ancient cracked tombstones—the place just teeming with ghosts and spooks of all kinds." He held up his hands and wiggled his fingers in a ghostlike way.

"What about it?" Paul asked, unimpressed.

"Now a minister, say, or an honest plumber, could walk through that cemetery and never be touched by a single spook, never see anything but the beauty of the moonlight, whereas…"

"Go on," I said.

"Someone with a tainted heart… a banker, say, or a

lawyer (this was aimed at Paul and me, of course) could walk by a downtown cemetery in broad daylight and feel a shudder of fear…"

"Bob has a new theory," I explained to Dave, "that bankers are parasites living off people's greed and lawyers are parasites living off their thirst for vengeance…"

"Whereas sports writers," Paul chimed in, "live off the innocent desire of people wanting to see men bash each other's heads in."

Bob laughed as he poured himself another beer. He looked ready to respond in kind, and probably would have if Dave hadn't said:

"I know of a case like that."

The serious tone of his voice arrested us.

"Like what?" Paul asked.

"A place where one man was haunted—and another saw nothing but beauty."

There was a moment's pause. We were suddenly aware of the silence in the house. Bob's voice sounded a little awkward when he spoke.

"Let's hear it," he said.

"I've told you what it's like in our part of Brazil. Twenty, thirty years ago it was mostly empty grasslands and jungle—a few settlements along the river, a few small farms. Then people began arriving. They were pioneers—poor, but scraping together a living on dirt farms and gradually building up their lives. After a while, as they settled in and their fruit trees began to produce, they began to live better. But it's a hard life.

"Then, ten or twelve years ago, land values went up and speculators started moving in. The original pioneers didn't have title to their land—they'd never heard of such things. They had legal rights because they'd occupied the land for over ten years, but they didn't know that. So rich men in São Paulo and Goiânia would mock up 'titles' to the land and their agents would go around to the poor hick pioneers and tell them they were on the rich man's land and they had to get off. Half the time, especially in the beginning, the poor fools would believe them. They'd sign the paper the agent told them to sign, gratefully accepting an 'indemnification' the agent handed them—maybe fifty bucks for thirty acres of land—and get dumped by the new owner's truck in the nearest town. Sometimes the new owner farmed the land; more often he let it sit vacant, increasing in value. Meanwhile, the pioneer and his family slowly starved in town—without money, land, or work, families began to fall apart. Kids died of malnutrition, the men drank, their sons got into trouble, their daughters—some of them—fell into prostitution."

Dave paused. His voice as he spoke had been dry, almost clinical. Only, if you knew him, you could hear the hard irony lying under the surface.

"That was bad enough. But some of the pioneers began to catch on—or were just plain stubborn—and wouldn't give up their land. So the rich men and their agents started to roughen up their tactics. They would work away at the weakest families—threatening them, pressuring them, until they sold. Then the more stubborn ones would be isolated—have you ever tried living out on a farm without any neighbors, with gunmen harassing you, burning your crops, threatening your family's lives? They got rid of a lot that way.

"In some places whole groups of families held out. Judges were bought and police came in and beat up the men and tried to force them to leave the land. But the people went to the Church, and the Church helped them organize and got them lawyers, and the people stayed on the land. Then their houses were burned and their leaders gunned down and—" Dave waved his hand, "—you know the rest."

We had read Dave's letters and knew something about it—the people struggling, the beatings, the murders.

"Out near the Araguaia River clinic, we had a guy who was particularly adept at getting people off the land. The people called him Tumbão, and he was a son-of-a-bitch....

"He was a local guy from one of the villages. He started out as a surveyor for the state, using that position to become a 'real estate agent,' which down there means a guy who uses every trick he can to buy land cheaply for the rich. After he'd put together some funds, he started to buy land for himself, though he kept on buying for rich outsiders too, earning fat commissions and political privileges.

"By the time I knew him, he was a very rich man. He was crude and gauche—a big man—handsome, I suppose, in his way, though he had a paunch that overhung his big leather belt. Like a lot of those guys, he wore expensive dude cowboy clothes—fancy shirts, blue jeans, boots, brass buckles—the whole bit.

"He must have been about fifty then. He had two grown sons—privileged, arrogant young men who had been raised to think that anything they wanted they could just take—land, women—whatever. He and his sons drove around in big pick-up trucks, the deluxe models with fancy upholstery and stripes painted on the sides and smoked glass windows. They spent hours at a sidewalk bar on the plaza in town, drinking with other landowners.

"The bar was right across from the church. Most of those guys have no time for the Church since it's come out in support of the poor. I remember one day I was coming out of mass when Tumbão called out to me from where he was lounging at one of the tables at the bar.

"'Hey, Doctor. Don't tell me *you* believe in all that stuff,' and he waved his hand toward the church.

"I stopped in the street and looked over at him. I wish I could tell you how much I hate him and all his kind—it's wrapped up for me, somehow, in that moment—in a tight, hard ball of hate. Sitting there, sleek and arrogant, drinking beer at two dollars a bottle—more than a man's wage for a day's labor—while the people they've stolen from are dead or dying of hunger, trapped in misery.

"'Yes,' I answered. 'I believe.'

"'And you're a man of science,' he said scornfully, as if he knew anything about it.

"'It's evident to everyone that you do *not* believe,' I said, and I walked off. But for once, perhaps, I was wrong about him.

"About two weeks later, they brought Tumbão into the clinic. The clinic is on the river, about fifty kilometers by dirt road from the town. Our jeep was driving out. There's a narrow wooden bridge over a creek not far from us. Tumbão's pick-up had missed the bridge and turned over. He was alone. He had managed to climb out of the truck and up to the road, where they found him, bleeding and almost unconscious.

"I was busy when they brought him in. One of our aides did what he could to bandage him and stop the bleeding. It's funny, you know: two of the men who brought him in and the aide were from families whose land he'd stolen."

Dave stopped for a moment and looked at his hands, stretching them open once or twice. Then he continued.

"Anyhow, when I got down to him, it was clear to me he was dying. I think it was clear to him too. He was conscious, and his eyes looked out from under his bandaged forehead like two terrified, hunted little animals. He reached out his hand toward me.

"'Doctor.' His voice was almost a whisper.

"'What do you want, Tumbão.'

"'Doctor... To tell you...'

"So I sat down beside him, and—gasping out in bits and pieces—he told me."

A scattering of small farmers in the region had managed to hold on to their land. One of these was Aristides Gomes. Partly because his land was a small triangle wedged between two large tracts, partly because he had been shrewd enough to register title before most small farmers even thought of doing so, Aristides' land had never been taken. He was a thin, slight, white-haired old man who rode a horse straight-backed and dignified. He and his wife, Antônia, lived on the farm.

When Tumbão was a young man, just starting out surveying for the state, he became a frequent visitor at Aristides and Antônia's farm. It was a beautiful spot—fertile fields, a farmhouse nestled on a green hill that sloped down to the Araguaia River, a small stream running down the slope close to the house. Whenever he arrived at the house, Dona Antônia would greet him with the customary greeting: "Enter, *compadre*. We have very little, but all that we have is yours."

For Tumbão had become their *compadre*—that is, they were godparents to one of his sons. This had happened early on, when Tumbão was a poor surveyor and Aristides and Antônia were among the most respected members of the community. To be a *compadre* is a sacred relationship, as binding as family ties.

Over the years, things changed. Money flowed into a few hands. Tumbão got rich; Aristides and Antônia maintained their farm lifestyle—their farm now one of a dozen or so small farms left in the region.

In his dealings, Tumbão gained control of one of the tracts of land bordering Aristides' farm, and the beauty of the farm began to obsess him. He imagined making his own home there—tearing down the old house and putting up a new one beside the stream and the small reservoir, on the slope overlooking the Araguaia. He offered Aristides a good price for the land—not just once, but pressing him time and again. The old man had no interest in selling.

Then one morning Aristides rode out on his horse and didn't come back. In the afternoon, his horse came home without him. Dona Antônia, desperate with worry, sent the two hired hands out looking. They found him, dead on the trail. Apparently he had fallen from his horse and hit his head on a rock. All his life he'd been riding, and the horse was well trained. A snake on the path, people said, but how many legs the snake had…. Who could tell?

Dona Antônia, at least, suspected nothing. In a land where people who want to kill someone just shoot him down, why suspect subterfuge? Police investigations wouldn't even cross her mind—the police are there to arrest drunks and force poor people off rich men's land. In the tropical heat, a man dies and is buried in twenty-four hours, and then is forgotten except for the candle-lit prayers of a few friends.

But she grieved. It was natural that her *compadre* would be nearby, and it was he who took her affairs in hand. A couple of weeks later, he suggested she should sell the farm and, after a few days, she agreed. He was to make a down payment and pay the rest in monthly installments—

he drew up a paper and she signed. She received the first payment and moved into town. When it came time for the second payment, she went around to Tumbão's office.

He wasn't in—he was a very busy man. But after several days, she found him and mentioned the payment.

"Payment, *comadre*?" he asked in his friendliest manner, laying a hand on her shoulder, a look of good natured puzzlement on his face. "But you must be mistaken. I've paid you what we agreed."

She looked up into his smiling face and understood completely. Whether—this time—he had committed murder: that thought didn't cross her mind. But her vision cleared completely, and she knew Tumbão for what he was. That knowing showed in her eyes.

"If you like, we can take a look at the contract, *comadre*, and see if I'm forgetting something..." His voice faltered.

She said nothing. She was illiterate, but she knew then what the document she had signed would say.

"Of course, if there's been a misunderstanding, *comadre*, I could perhaps manage to pay you a little bit more. Times are hard..."

Again she said nothing. She looked at him, knowing him at last through and through, then turned and walked away. She spoke of it to no one, holding her knowledge in her heart, although everyone knew. Within two months she died.

But her eyes haunted Tumbão. In them he saw himself reflected—saw who he was—and he was scared. He threw himself restlessly into activity, managing his accounts in the bank, supervising the marketing of his cattle, and most of the time forgetting the look in Dona Antônia's eyes. But if he paused during the day, or if he tried to sleep before he was completely exhausted, that look would come back to him.

It was ridiculous, he thought. What he had done with Dona Antônia wasn't half as bad as the things most landowners did—wasn't half as bad as things he himself had done. He hadn't threatened her—outwitted her, perhaps, but that was business. Why should this one thing bother him?

In the end he decided to confront it. He had been avoiding going up to Arisitides' old farmstead, but he decided that the only way to put the devil to rest—that was the phrase he used—was to go up there and start planning the new house.

So one morning he drove his pick-up out to the farmstead. He got there about ten o'clock, a time he had often dropped by in the old days. He stopped the truck, but sat inside it for a few minutes, reluctant to get out. The place looked as it always did—beautiful, the flowering trees blooming, the fields falling gently down toward the Araguaia. But Dona Antônia's eyes haunted his memory.

He shook himself and got out of the pick-up, slamming its door behind him. The loud, hard, metallic sound of the door slamming was comforting and familiar, breaking the quiet of the place. He laughed aloud at his own misgivings and started toward the house.

As he walked he set his mind on looking at the farmstead not as a place but as *property*—the fencing here would have to be fixed at so much cost, materials and labor; the drainage ditch rerouted. He was in his element now, holding things where he understood them, and it was with a comfortable feeling of control that he unlocked the wooden door and stepped into the house.

Suddenly he wanted to turn and run. His heart shrieked fear, but his body stood still, unable to move. In the shadows of the house—after the bright tropical sunlight—he could see very little. He stood like a terrified animal, peering into the darkness as his eyes adjusted to the gray light. He started to breathe more easily, berating himself for being carried away by fear. Yet he felt as if a net held him—he could not turn and leave.

Then he saw her. Dona Antônia. She was seated at the table, where he'd seen her so often before. He was not sure how he perceived her, whether it was really with his eyes or simply with his heart, but that she was there he could not doubt. She was looking at him as she had looked at him in the old days, but the look cut through him.

"Welcome, *compadre*," she said.

He felt the net dragging him forward, and suddenly he understood that it was the same net, the net of hospitality, that had been woven when he was here so often before. He shuddered and tried to shake himself loose from it, and he heard laughter—strange, taunting, hollow laughter—and realized with horror that the laughter was coming from himself.

The figure before him was standing now and reaching out her hand. Against his will he reached out his own hand and took hers, and he felt a terrifying chill sweep through his body.

"Come, *compadre*, sit down." It was the old ritual and he had to follow it. He sat on a hard wooden chair, knowing what was coming, powerless to resist it. Then she said the words that he had been fearing—fearing for a long time.

"We have very little, *compadre*, but what we have is yours."

He seemed then to drink into himself her broken heart, her disillusion, to see his own deception, see himself in her eyes. This he had nearly been prepared for, and he was feeling almost relieved that it was going to be over, that he could go now. Then the figure said again, "We have very little, *compadre*, but what we have is yours." She turned and motioned, and another figure came forward.

It was Jonas Luis, one of the first farmers he'd defrauded years ago—he'd almost forgotten him—and Jonas Luis came forward repeating the words: "We have very little, *compadre*, but what we have is yours." And Tumbão drank in all Jonas Luis' self-hate at having been weak and foolish, all the bitterness of having been taken advantage of, the self-scorn that led to drink, the torture of alcoholic death. After Jonas Luis came Fátima, his daughter, who had become a prostitute—and she said: "We have very little, *compadre*, but what we have is yours." And he took into himself the feelings of a woman's body being used, abused, discarded, vanity and self-loathing corroding the soul, body wracked with venereal disease, wasting away to emaciation and death.

Then, one by one, came children, and each one said, "We have very little, *compadre*..." and they gave him the stomach wrenching cramps of hunger, of killing dysentery, of little illnesses—measles, colds—bringing death to underfed bodies, of their childish wondering that life could be cruel. Then young Sebastião, son of Salomão, whose land Tumbão had taken—Sebastião—who had moved to the city slums and been killed there in gang wars: "We have very little, *compadre*..." and he gave Tumbão the rage of the streets, the anger of the trapped.

Still they continued to come, one by one, the men he had stolen from or killed, their bitter wives, their children. The prostitutes he'd had, the workers he'd abused, even his own dead wife among them. And each said "We have very little, *compadre*..." and each gave all he had given them. He looked up and saw more coming—hundreds—and through an insane act of will he opened his mouth and screamed, lifted his heavy arms and broke the net, rose up, turning toward the door and stumbling out. He burst into sunlight and saw that all the beauty of the place had turned to terror: the flowering bushes dripped as though with blood, the branches of the trees were blanched skeletons, the yard was ragged with rocks like claws, the blades of grass grew sharp and cutting. He ran toward the cushioned safety of his pick-up, climbed in and fumbled with the ignition. He could feel the figures in the house coming toward him—he would not look back. The ignition sputtered, then caught, and he jerked the truck forward quickly, picking up speed, escaping, free.

It was three kilometers down the road that they found him, crashed.

There was utter silence. Then Paul cleared his throat.

"I see what you mean," he said. "About it being like Bob said... the evil soul seeing that place as ugly..."

He trailed off, caught in the inadequacy of his own words.

For a moment Dave said nothing. His eyes were abstracted, far away, as if seeing something all-absorbing, as though there were more that he had to tell.

"Yes," he said at last. His voice was tired. "It's like Bob said. A few weeks later, I went by the farmstead with Frei Aloísio—I don't think I know anyone better humored, more willing to fight injustice, more pure-hearted than Aloísio. All he could do was praise the beauty of the place. But I..." he paused a moment... "I could see something different."

"You?" I exclaimed, surprised.

Again he was silent, his eyes searching out memories.

"Yes. I could see the beauty Aloísio was talking about. But I could also see something else—a shadow of the terror Tumbão had seen."

"But why…?" Bob started to ask.

Dave turned to him. "It's just as you said. It's all in the purity of heart…"

"What are you saying?" I asked.

"In the clinic, Tumbão told me his story. His heavy, arrogant face had turned into fat, blubbering fear. He looked at me, his eyes begging comfort, and I was filled with disgust and hate and bitterness—at him, at everything he stood for, at all he and his kind have done to the people. I turned my hardness against his need to be comforted. I whispered to him, 'You'd better watch out, Tumbão—those spirits can come even here.'

"It was a childish thing to say. Yet, strangely, as soon as I said it, I felt a shiver run down my spine and a chill brush against me. Tumbão's eyes focused to my left above my shoulder, as if someone were standing there, and he started to scream. He grabbed for my hand, but I pulled away, stood up, and walked out. He was still screaming. Chico, the aide, was standing in the hall. 'We have plenty of other things to do, Chico,' I said. 'Let's get to work.'

"'Yes, Doctor,' he answered. But I know that he and the others went in to watch Tumbão—try to comfort him—as soon as my back was turned. They're gentle people—what can you expect?

"I went around, making myself very busy. I could hear Tumbão screaming in the other wing, and I steeled myself against it, working harder. After a few minutes, Chico came to me.

"'Doctor Davíd,' he said. '*Seu* Tumbão is calling for the priest. Can we send the jeep into town?'

"By jeep it's about a forty minute ride into town over a rough dirt road. I knew Aloísio was there. I was sitting at my desk and I picked up a pile of reports.

"'No,' I said without looking up. 'We may need the jeep.'

"Chico stood there silently. I could sense his discomfort, but I kept looking at the reports.

"'But, Doctor,' he said hesitantly. 'He wants to confess...'

"'No,' I said again, this time looking right at him.

"He opened his mouth as if to speak, but then turned and went out of the room.

"For the next couple of hours I sat at my desk, pretending to myself that I was working. Through it all I could hear the screams of the dying man, screams of torture. They told me later he kept saying, 'No more,' motioning with his arms as if pushing people away. His eyes were glazed over, but now and then he would focus on one of the nurses and beg for the priest.

"Later I learned that one of the kids—another one whose family had lost their land—got on his bike and rode the fifty kilometers into town. But by the time Aloísio got there, it was too late."

There was an uncomfortable silence. Then Paul spoke.

"But what you said—about needing the jeep. That was perfectly reasonable."

"All excuses are reasonable," Dave said after a moment. "But I knew... Chico knew... we all knew that for anyone else the jeep would have been sent. It didn't go for one reason—one reason only: Hate."

"That seems to me reason enough," I said.

"Does it?" Dave turned his eyes on me—eyes startlingly abstracted, haunted.

"I denied that man reconciliation," he said. "I denied it because I hated him. The evil had entered into me too. I hoped—to this day I hope—that he's burning in hell."

He stood up suddenly, restlessly, looking off at something distant, not in the room. He was sweating, and for a moment I thought of Connie's comment about Moses' bush and saw the fire slowly eating him away. The silence in the room was suffocating, and when he spoke it was far away and almost a whisper.

"May God have mercy on my soul."

CLÁUDIO
(Northern Goiás, 1986)

1

There were three men in the jeep, and he wasn't even the handsomest. They stopped to drink water. The other two went back to the jeep, but he stayed for a few moments in the cool front room of the thatched roofed adobe farmhouse, drinking more water dipped in an aluminum cup from the clay pot. He had dark hair, light skin, clean finger nails; his eyes and face looked sensitive, and suddenly Maria das Dores felt embarrassed, aware of her dusty bare feet and the small bulge of the child in her belly beneath her faded blue dress.

"I didn't know anyone would be stopping," she said, "or I wouldn't look so messy." Her hand went up and pushed back a wisp of light brown hair from her temple. His eyes alighted on her and he smiled.

"You shouldn't worry about that," he said. "You're very pretty."

It was a light compliment, she knew, the kind men from the city make easily. Yet he'd said it, and his eyes looked as if he'd meant it.

"Cláudio," one of the other men shouted from the jeep. "Let's go!"

The brown palm-straw broom set aside; dust still rising from where she'd swept the dirt floor, hazing the afternoon sunlight. Carefully, she set the small chipped mirror on the wooden table and looked into it. Hazel eyes, smooth browned skin, small nose, square chin. Pretty — they'd all said she was pretty when she was seventeen, but that was five years and three children ago, and who ever said she was pretty now? Except this afternoon...

João sat silently on the stool, eating his supper, one huge hand cradling the tin plate, the other clutching the spoon as it dug into the rice and beans and shoveled them into his mouth. Click of the spoon on the plate, whish of lifting, chewing; click of the spoon on the plate, whish of lifting, chewing.

She lay awake in the hammock, sleepless in the black night. Cláudio. They'd called out his name, Cláudio. He would be standing in the front room. He would reach out and gently touch her cheek.

The small statue of Our Lady of Aparecida stood on the tiny wooden shelf against the bare adobe brick wall, her black face looking sightlessly at Maria das Dores, her black hands held palms forward, her blue robe decked with glass jewels.

"Mother of God," Maria das Dores whispered. "Mother of God..."

2

Pretty, they said she was, the day at Colher she'd been a bride: Maria das Dores, the prettiest of the brides. There had been seven couples getting married in the clearing under the giant mango tree; the priest came through on his yearly visit and everyone for miles around was there. Seventeen years old, and João standing beside her, twenty-five, independent with his five alqueires of land, large and strong and quiet, handsome.

Sometimes Cláudio would come in the day time — whether it was morning or early afternoon she could never decide — driving over the hill in the jeep, alone. He would step out of the jeep and close its door behind him, looking up the little slope to the farmhouse, and she would be standing in the front door. She would be wearing her best dress — the white one with pink flowers — and would have just bathed — but how could that be if it were still only early afternoon? — but maybe she was going out somewhere special. She wasn't heavy — was the baby born already? — but that would be months away. Maybe she was heavy still, but he didn't mind, he thought she was pretty anyway — and he would walk hesitatingly up the slope, looking at her with sensitive, kind eyes, and a few feet away he would stop, and they would look at each other and he would softly say, "das Dores" — but how could he say that? He didn't know her name. He would have asked. At some other farmhouse he and his friends would have stopped and he would have mentioned that they'd passed by a little farm on a hill, and the people would say, "that must be João and das Dores," then would go on, the way country people do, to talk about them. Cláudio would listen. "She was one of the prettiest girls around," "She had the best marks in her class the year she graduated," — but that would only be fourth grade, maybe he wouldn't like that — "She's a good wife and a fine mother...." He would listen, outwardly calm but fascinated inside. So he'd know her name, and he'd reach out and touch her cheek....

"The rice will be ready to harvest next week," João said. "I'll be trading work days with Zé Farias and Sebastião. I'll have to take food."

Sometimes João had died. It would be all right then. He'd died—maybe just died, of a heart attack. He'd go to heaven because he was a good man. She was a widow. It was the seventh day and she was at the cemetery with everyone there. They were all thinking, "Poor das Dores, what is she going to do, alone with two children and another on the way?" Or maybe "with three children"—yes, the baby would be born and in her arms and she wouldn't be heavy. They'd hear the jeep drive up, and the others would look because cars weren't very common here—they wouldn't recognize the young man getting out of the jeep. Das Dores wouldn't look, she'd be praying, but she'd know who it was. She'd turn away from the grave and he'd be standing there, hesitantly, not knowing if she felt what he felt. And his eyes would look into her eyes....

"I'm going to chain one of the dogs down in the lower field," João said. "The wild pigs are getting at the manioc crop."

"Das Dores," he would say, and he'd reach out and touch her cheek—but how could he do that there at the cemetery with all those people around? No, it would be later when she was back at the house, her mother and sister helping inside, and she would have stepped out the front door as she saw him walking up toward the house. He'd touch her cheek and say, "das Dores," looking at her with those caring eyes—yet with passion in his eyes, passion held in, controlled because he loved her. She'd look down at the ground and say softly, "Cláudio," and he'd know she'd been thinking of him and the words would come tumbling out of his mouth—how he'd thought of her since that day he'd stopped for water, how he'd stayed away because he knew she was married, but then he'd heard just yesterday and he'd come as quickly as he could—he loved her, he wanted to take care of her and the children, he wanted... "Cláudio, not now," she would say. She was just newly a widow, she needed time. He would wait for her, he would say—could she only give him a promise? And she would look into his eyes and whisper, "Yes."

"Pedro and I are going this morning to slaughter his steer."

The slow silence of empty hours alone in the house.

"Mother of God..." It's not real, Maria das Dores. "Mother of God, I know it's not real. But what else do I have?"

3

He would almost always be in the house now, and her life rotated around him. She cleaned the four rooms with extra spirit, sweeping the dirt floor, dusting the few pieces of rough wooden furniture, decorating the house with flowers and green branches, with pictures from a magazine her mother had once brought back from Goiania, singing to herself happily, showing him what a good wife she could be; taking care of the babies with joy, conscious of his eyes on her. She wouldn't let him know, of course, that she was thinking of him; she made special meals for João and got herself pretty for him when he came home, greeting him warmly—after all, *he* would be watching. Let him envy João a little, thinking how lucky João was to have such a wife. Let *him* want her for *his* wife. Some day, some how, it would happen. But for now, let him be a little envious.

She lay awake in the hammock. Cláudio would have wanted to kiss her that afternoon; she'd turned her face away, but he'd held her strong and close in his arms, and she would have stayed there a moment before she pushed him away.

Now she felt him near. His face was close to hers, and his finger reached out and stroked her cheek. "Maria das Dores, I love you," he said. She reached up and held his hand in hers, then felt his other hand gently touching her shoulder, her breast, her side, her thigh....

"Mother of God, help me," she whispered. She shifted in her hammock and stared into the black empty darkness of the room.

4

After supper she talked to João, loving—laughing and alive—flushed with joy—weaving little incidents of the day into a bright tapestry of words, because she knew—although João couldn't—that *he* would be there watching them.

João's dark eyes followed her as she moved around the kitchen, reflecting her liveliness.

"So I picked the baby up, and there he was with yellow flowers clutched in his hand..."

"Das Dores." João was looking at her.

She went over and sat on a stool near him, looking at him, attentive. *He* would want a wife like that, to listen to him when he came home.

João reached out and took her hand in his big, callused hand. He looked down, tracing the toe of his sandal along the dirt floor.

"This afternoon..." His lips were searching for words; he was always slow to talk. "Right almost at night fall... the sunlight... it was on the rice. It made it look all gold. I thought..."

He stopped talking, and his eyes came up to her eyes.

"Do you ever feel a kind of ... heaviness?"

For an instant she was startled, thinking of the baby bulging in her belly.

5

"Did you see how pretty das Dores is," she overheard Dona Lúcia say to Tia Ana outside the kitchen as the wedding dancers whirled by. And later, old Chico Pardo, half drunk, had lifted up his arms and shouted, "She's the prettiest of the brides." And Maria das Dores had been embarrassed because she knew it was true.

When was it that she stopped wanting João to touch her? Not at first. At first she *queria ele bem* — as people said — wanted him a lot. They spent days together, laughing, working, playing, making love. But then came the bad harvest, and the babies, and the long hot days. She noticed how sweaty and dirty he was, how hard his hands were. He talked of fields and corn and pigs. When he wanted her, he wanted her hard, dropping right off to sleep in the hammock. When she was pregnant, though, she could get him mostly to leave her alone.

She was restless in the hammock, half hoping, half afraid Cláudio would come. He would touch her cheek and whisper, "Maria das Dores, I love you." His hand would gently touch her breast, pass over her stomach, touch her thigh....

She felt a hand touch her in the dark—a big hard hand—João, driven—she knew—by his need for her—and her body alive and ready and waiting. She reached up and pulled him toward her.

João looked at her, standing in the kitchen doorway in the morning light. Something in his eyes, something new, or maybe something from a long time ago.
He said, "Maria das Dores..."
"What is it?"
Silence. Chickens clucking; breeze rustling palm leaves.
"Nothing."
He turned and walked down toward the fields.

Sometimes Cláudio would arrive silently in the afternoon when she was all alone. She would somehow know he was coming—and what he would want—but still....

"Mother of God, help me."
Look out the window, Maria das Dores.
She rose and went to the window and looked down the gentle slope to where the fields lay. She saw João struggling up the path, stooped under the weight of a full sack of rice—saw him startlingly clearly, as if all the air between them were crystal glass: his bare feet, his torn trousers, his home spun shirt. And for the first time she saw an old man within the young one: hands hard with labor, face lined with worry, body crooked with heavy loads.
"Mother of God," she whispered. "Forgive me."

6
Still, it took four days to do what she had to do.
It was a moonlit night, and she went out into the back

yard to a place at the split rail fence. She knew *he* would be on the other side, where the pasture sloped down gently, open and free.

She stopped by the fence and listened, listened to the night sounds of the land, the insects singing, the distant chee of a monkey.

She spoke out loud.

"Goodbye, Cláudio."

He would understand. He would always understand.

"Goodbye," she said again, and she saw him turn and go walking down the hill. She stood for a moment more, then started back to the farmhouse where her husband lay in his hammock, snoring, fast asleep.

STONE

(Western Bahia, 1934–1964)

I

In 1934, the young war lord, Epitácio dos Santos, then only in his mid-twenties but already a strong force in the mountains of central Bahia, granted to Domingos Pereira, a gunman who had served his family for many years, the use of certain lands in the far western part of the state. The only condition of the grant was that every five years Domingos and his heirs would sign a writ acknowledging Colonel Epitácio's ownership of the land.

Old Domingos moved west to the land with his three young sons. It was rough country, with cattle spread over a vast area and scattered fields farmed by sharecroppers. But Domingos was a tough man and raised his sons to be tough.

As long as Domingos was alive, there was no problem with the signing of the writ. Every five years a messenger would arrive from Colonel Epitácio. It was a long ride, sixteen days by horseback and, later, three or four days by jeep over a round-about patchwork of bad dirt roads. Old Domingos would greet the messenger as an honored guest, ordering a young steer slaughtered, and sending off boys on horseback to call in the hands, sharecroppers, and the few neighbors in that sparse country. He would sign the document right away, then would sit in the shade of a mango tree and chat with the messenger, asking about happenings back east. When the steer was roasted, the gathering would eat and drink *cachaça* until long after the sun had set, and the kerosene lanterns flickered late into the night.

The first time after Domingos' death the messenger arrived on horseback, he received no greeting. Leônidas, the eldest son, walked out of the rough, rambling palm-thatched house that was the family's headquarters. He was a glowering, powerful man with thick black hair, built like a bull but with a way of holding his arms slightly forward and away from his body, like an ape, as though his arm muscles were too large to let his arms hang straight.

"What do you want?" He spoke as though the messenger were not expected, although he and his brothers had been watching the calendar for weeks.

"I'm here with Colonel Epitacio's papers."

The second brother, Mauro, had come out of the house. He was as tall as Leônidas, but not as thick and muscular. At first glance he was handsome—a high forehead, light brushed-back hair—until the messenger looked in his eyes. Those eyes were arresting—would be fascinating to young girls and other prey. After a moment the messenger tore his own eyes away from Mauro's eyes; he had seen something crazed and cruel there.

"Listen..." Mauro started. His voice was higher than expected, crazed in the same way his eyes were crazed. Leônidas held up his powerful hand and Mauro stopped talking.

"Dismount," Leônidas said, "and come inside."

The messenger got down from his horse and stepped through the low door of the house. It took a moment for his eyes to adjust to the darkness inside. Then he saw the dirt floor, the rough square table, the small rawhide-covered stools, the bare adobe brick walls. There was nothing here to show that these men were vice-regents over a vast domain of lands, nothing of the cool grace of Colonel Epitácio's house back east. But the messenger was used to such places where men of wealth lived in stark, almost furnitureless rough houses, working in old rough clothes, sleeping in hammocks.

"Let me see the papers," Leônidas said.

The messenger extracted two pieces of paper from his leather pouch and handed them to Leônidas. The powerful hand took the papers, looking—the messenger thought—as though it would like to crumple and crush them. But Leônidas held the sheets close to his face and laboriously read them.

There was a coughing in the corner and the messenger became aware of another man, hunched on a stool in the shadows against the wall. The man spat on the floor. This was the third brother, Antenor. In four years he would be dead of tuberculosis, leaving an infant son.

Leônidas laid the papers on the table.

"You have something to write with?" he asked the messenger.

"But..." Mauro started.

"Be quiet," Leônidas said.

The messenger took a fountain pen out of his pouch, removed the cap, and handed the pen to Leônidas. The big hand clutched it and slowly, painfully, scratched out a signature at the bottom margin of the second sheet.

"Mauro," Leônidas said.

His brother came reluctantly over to the table, as though pulled against his will, a roped yearling. He stood for a moment, then moving quickly, grabbed the pen and wrote his name.

"Antenor," Leônidas said.

The third brother got up from his stool and moved languidly over to the table. He was emaciated, half a ghost already, indifferent. He signed, his signature a smooth, well-formed flourish.

Leônidas picked up the papers. "There," he said, holding them out to the messenger. The messenger folded them carefully and put them in his pouch.

There was no offer of a meal, of *cachaça*, or coffee. Not even a cup of water.

The messenger nodded to them, turned, walked out of the house, mounted and rode away.

The second time following the death of Domingos, when the messenger arrived, the brothers refused to sign.

"What am I to tell Colonel Epitácio?" the messenger asked.

Leônidas spat on the ground.

Five more years passed.

Again a messenger arrived, a new messenger. Again the brothers refused to sign.

The messenger spoke up, reminding them of the original grant, of the law.

Leônidas brought up his huge right arm and swung it, backhanding the messenger's face. The messenger reeled and fell against the wall, his face bruised, his mouth bleeding.

"Tell your boss that," Leônidas said.

Another five years passed.

A third messenger came. He was a man of courage, capable of taking care of himself, but he hesitated as he rode up toward the house. It was mid-morning and a small group stood gathered in front of the house, talking about work. They turned to look at the messenger.

Leônidas was there, and Mauro, and half a dozen of their men, men toughened by rough land and cattle and keeping sharecroppers in line.

"Leônidas Pereira?" the messenger asked, dismounting.

Leônidas nodded without speaking.

"I have a letter from Colonel Epitácio," the messenger said. He pulled it out of his pouch, unfolded it, and handed it to Leônidas.

Leônidas took the letter and read it. He read slowly, painfully, sounding out the words with his lips. He would not have listened to the words of a messenger, but the written words of the Colonel still had the power to hold him. He finished the letter and handed it to Mauro.

Mauro read quickly, restlessly. An expression of irritation crossed his face. He crumpled the letter and threw it on the ground.

"He thinks he can scare us?" he said.

"He writes the truth," the messenger said calmly.

Mauro moved forward rapidly as if to hit him, and the messenger thrust up an arm to protect himself. His arm brushed against Mauro, who recoiled. Leônidas stepped up and grabbed the messenger, then swung his fist and hit him in the stomach. The blow seemed to let loose deep anger in the brothers, and they both closed in on the messenger, hitting him until he fell. Leônidas kicked him, and would have kicked him again if one of his own men hadn't held him back. Leônidas looked down at the injured figure on the ground, grunted, then turned and walked back into the house. Mauro spat once, then followed his brother.

Silence hung like mist in the cool, high-ceilinged library of the old mansion. The dark red floor-tile glowed. A beam of sunlight fell from one of the tall windows, across the dark red floor.

"I have been patient with these people long enough."

"You have twenty years before they gain rights to the land, Colonel," his assistant said. "Fifteen have already passed."

"You think it's the land I care about?" The Colonel turned and called to his son, who was seated at the far end of the room.

"Amado, I want you to take care of this."

His son stood up. He was of medium height with dark hair and eyes, light brown skin.

"As you wish, Father."

"Take as many men as you need."

The Colonel turned and walked out of the room, his boots hard against the tile floor.

II

Tonico saw the jeep winding down the rough dirt road into the valley from the east. He could hear the distant whine of its motor, the pauses as it shifted gears. Automobiles were still rare out here and his seventeen-year-old heart beat faster with excitement. And fear. There was always fear there.

"What is it?"

The rough voice of his Uncle Leônidas, who had come out of the house behind him.

"A jeep, *tio*."

"I can see that." His uncle stood, looking sullenly up at the road, powerful and strong. For all Tonico's life, this man had been the strength and power of the family. Tonico depended on him and was afraid of him. Not the way he was afraid of *Tio* Mauro, who might strike out any time at any one, like a cold blade—like the blade of the knife he always carried in his boot. Tonico feared Leônidas as one might be afraid of a huge mountain that shadowed one's home, making it small and insignificant.

"It means no good," Leônidas said. "Go call Mauro and the men."

The boy started around the house to call his other uncle, but the sound of the approaching jeep had been heard, and he met his uncle and five men coming in from the field. Mauro pushed Tonico aside and walked over to Leônidas. They watched the jeep in silence.

"Some bastard coming from Epitácio," Mauro said after a moment.

Leônidas nodded.

The jeep had reached the large wooden cattle gate that blocked the road. The jeep stopped, its motor idling, and a man got out of the driver's seat, opened the gate, stepped back to the jeep.

"He's alone," Mauro said softly.

Leônidas grunted and turned to the men.

"Go back to work," he said.

The men moved off, reluctantly, held by curiosity but unable to disobey Leônidas' order. Tonico stayed where he was.

The jeep was drawing closer now. It came to a stop about twenty meters in front of them. The motor switched off, and the stranger got out.

Sometimes Tonico dreamed. He wouldn't have let his uncles know, but he dreamed. Not usually sleeping, but in the day, pausing over his hoe in the fields, or in the evening, sitting in the kitchen and watching the fire on the open clay stove. Things his uncles would not understand.

They were not clear dreams. They were vague, touching an emptiness that Tonico did not know how to describe, but that was sometimes suddenly, terrifyingly there.

Somehow the stranger fit into these dreams. He

hadn't been there, then suddenly he was, as though he had always been. He was ordinary looking enough, friendly and open-faced—dark eyes, light brown skin, a little better dressed than the men Tonico knew. It was nothing special, yet the stranger was there, fitting somehow into the dreams.

"Who are you?" *Tio* Leônidas was saying.

"Amado dos Santos," the stranger said lightly. "Epitácio's son." He came forward and held out his hand in greeting.

Slowly, reluctantly, Leônidas' huge hand reached out to take the stranger's. They shook hands. The stranger turned to Mauro, and Mauro also shook hands, but Tonico could sense the hate in him, as though by touching the stranger he was touching a poisonous snake. Then the stranger reached over and shook Tonico's hand, and Tonico felt warmth and peace there.

"I come from my father about the land."

The stranger was seated on a stool at the rough wooden table, Leônidas and Mauro seated across the table from him, Tonico leaning his stool two-legged against the wall.

"Our land," Mauro muttered.

The stranger turned, looking briefly at Tonico, then at Mauro. He had dark, clear eyes that seemed to look through one.

"Is it?" the stranger asked, his voice calm, almost gentle.

He and Mauro looked at each other, Mauro tense, defiant. Then Mauro suddenly lowered his gaze and his body shuddered, as though he were cold. Tonico had never seen his uncle lower his eyes before anyone except Leônidas. He colored, sensing Mauro's humiliation. Then he sensed something else emerging from the humiliation, a snake sliding out of the broken, plowed earth, waiting to strike. But Mauro did not yet lift his head.

"My brother means that we have worked this land most our lives," Leônidas said. He shifted his big frame on the wooden stool. "It would have no value without what we have done."

"No value?"

"Very little."

The stranger nodded, not so much in agreement, Tonico thought, but just acknowledging that he had heard. "No one says that you have to leave the land. Only that you respect the agreement your father made with mine."

Mauro's head shot up. "Who is your father to…"

"Silence," Leônidas commanded, his huge hand lifted.

The room fell silent. A tense silence. Outside Tonico could hear the chirp of insects. In the room he could hear breathing—Leônidas' heavy breathing, Mauro's sharper and shallower, the stranger's gentle and calm. And his own breathing, Tonico realized, half-suspended, and his own heart beating.

"What do you want from us?" Leônidas finally asked.

The stranger took out a folded sheet of paper. He unfolded it and laid it flat on the table, smoothing it with his hand. A strong, able hand.

"All of this," he said, making an inclusive motion, "was given to you by my father. His only condition has been that you acknowledge that. Three times you have refused to do so. This time he wants you to."

Again there was silence.

"My brother and I will discuss this," Leônidas said.

"I don't believe there is anything to discuss," the stranger answered.

"Nonetheless," Leônidas answered, "we will discuss it."

"All right." The stranger stood up. "I'll wait outside."

The tense silence remained in the room after the stranger stepped outside. From his stool by the wall, the boy watched his two uncles, still seated at the table. To them, he knew, he was essentially invisible, and he preferred it that way. To be noticed by his uncles, he had learned long ago, often led to unpleasant results. He sat quietly on his stool.

Leônidas motioned to Mauro and Mauro stood up and walked across the dirt floor to the open door. He looked out, then turned around and came back.

"He's over by the jeep," he said.

Leônidas nodded. Mauro sat down again, and leaned forward, his forearms on the table.

"Why did you say we'd discuss it?" he demanded, his voice querulous. "Why didn't you just tear it... "

His words drifted off like wind hitting against the mountain of his brother's bulk. Leônidas sat silent for a moment.

"You're always in a hurry," he said at last, looking at his brother. "Why are you rushing?"

"If you don't do a thing right away... if you think about it... sometimes you don't do it."

Leônidas stared at his brother. His face was expressionless, yet Tonico felt scorn underneath. Except when his bottled-up rage broke loose, his Uncle Leônidas never did anything impulsively. If he set on doing something, time and delay made little difference to his will. The thing would get done.

"We *have* discussed this," Mauro went on. His voice was high, emotional. "If we sign now, we're just giving them more time. Do you think they want us on this land? If we hold out a little longer, they'll have no claim."

Leônidas nodded. "We didn't know he would send his son," he said.

"What difference..." Mauro started to say, but then broke off. He stood up suddenly and walked over to the door, looking out. When he turned back into the room, his face was transformed—thinner looking, the jaw muscles tensed, his eyes bright but narrowed.

"You should see him standing there beside his jeep," he hissed, "the *filho de papai*. It must be nice to be the colonel's son, to never have to sweat your hide off over a piece of stinking land..."

He sat down. Leônidas said nothing.

"You're thinking," Mauro went on, "he's the only son. You're thinking that if his father dies without an heir, the matter will be tied up in the courts for years, like it always is... that nobody will give a damn about this land way out here."

"Don't be stupid," Leônidas said.

Mauro laughed, straightening himself on his stool and pushing back slightly from the table. The two brothers stared at each other.

Through the open door, Tonico saw the stranger come into view, walking toward them.

"He's coming back," he said.

The stranger stood in the doorway.

"We will call you when we want you," Leônidas said, rising to his feet.

"You've had enough time." The stranger's voice was quiet, firm.

Mauro stood up rapidly. "Enough time!" his voice was pitched high. "Enough time for you to..."

The stranger only glanced at Mauro, then looked at Leônidas.

"You know you need to sign..."

What happened seemed to Tonico to happen very slowly, though it took only seconds. It seemed to him that he had always known it would happen, that it had been set to happen from the beginning of time and yet, strangely, that he could have stopped it if he had wanted to, if he had only known how.

Mauro snaked his hand down to his boot. It came up sharply, holding the naked knife, striking quickly and silently toward the stranger's ribs. The stranger began to bring his arm forward, but too late, and Tonico saw the stranger's deep, clear eyes looking at him—at Tonico. And Tonico saw in those eyes a deep desire to forgive, waiting for him—waiting for Tonico—to accept being forgiven.

III

Leônidas had gone out and given the men tasks that would keep them far from the house. But the brothers waited until it was dark before they took the body out of the house, Tonico helping them to carry it. Fiddling with the keys, swearing under his breath, Leônidas got the motor started and jerked the jeep forward, turning and heading out the gate they held open for him, switching on the lights and moving up the slope eastward, as the stranger would have done were he driving himself home.

Tonico walked back to the house with Mauro. His uncle did not speak, but Tonico sensed anger, bitter hate, churning in Mauro, turning inward before—sometime, but not tonight—it would spew out again. His uncle went off toward the back of the house and Tonico went into the room where he—Tonico—slept: a barren little room with a dirt floor and a single wooden window, closed against the night air. He dropped into his hammock and lay looking up into the dark.

Though he had held the dead body in his arms, he had an odd sense that the stranger was alive, those clear eyes looking at him, that he would see him again. He shook himself with a slight shudder. He would dismiss the stranger from his mind.

So he did. Leônidas returned before daylight. No word was said but Tonico knew that somewhere, far from their land, the jeep would be found. There would be no body.

Murder in this rough back country was common. Murderers were seldom discovered, seldom punished.

All that day and all the next and all the weeks to come Tonico fenced the stranger out of his thoughts, not letting him into any corner of his mind. He rose early, went about his work, spoke little, obeyed his uncles. He was as he had always been. Except the nights that he awoke sweating from a dream, hearing the hooves of the war lord's army sweeping across the land.

A Hero for the People
(Southern Pará, 1988)

1

Old Father Gil refused to leave the Barreira das Almas mission on the Araguaia River. The Belgian priest was eighty-seven and as stubborn as a fence post. He would die, he said, serving the people he had served for twenty-five years.

Officially, the Council of his Order could have required him to return to the provincial house in Rio de Janeiro where most of the retired priests lived. But the superior, who was little more than half Father Gil's age and had been his student many years before, could not see his way to invoking the rule of obedience.

What could the Council do? Both the rules of the Order and common sense dictated that they couldn't leave the old priest alone. But Barreira das Almas was an out-of-the-way, decaying place in the eastern Amazon, never important but even less so now that road traffic had replaced boats: a slow, lifeless village on the banks of a slow, meandering river, plagued by periodic floods, its population moving out, so that a third of its houses stood empty and gradually disintegrating under the heavy

rains of the wet season and the dusty winds of the dry
season. How could the Order spare men needed for the
teeming slums of Rio de Janeiro and São Paulo?

It was then that someone remembered Brother Michel.
The Belgian brother had taken care of the Order's library
for the twenty-some years since he had arrived in Brazil.
But a young Brazilian brother had just earned a degree
in library science and was updating the old collection of
books and periodicals. Brother Michel was at loose ends.

It was a perfect solution. Brother Michel could go up
north and be a companion to the old man and then,
when Father Gil died, they could close the mission and
they would find something else for Brother Michel
somewhere.

So, on a hot, dry afternoon in July, when the bus from
Paraíso do Norte stopped on the dirt main street of
Barreira das Almas, a short stocky figure got out: balding,
thick glasses, barely five feet tall. After the bus conductor
handed him his heavy black bag, Brother Michel turned
to look at the bedraggled houses of his new home, his
face wearing a look of utter bewilderment.

In Rio de Janeiro, Brother Michel had developed the
custom, unnoticed by his superiors, of walking out in the
late afternoon or early evening, after his tasks in the
library were finished, to visit the poor in the neighborhood around the Order's center house. These were not
the poor of the community movements and the unions,
the poor who are struggling for the reign of God and
justice on earth. These were the complaining poor,
cramped into the rooms of old run-down mansions, one
or two families to a room—the poor with aching backs
and rheumatism and drunken husbands, who
remembered a lost chance early in life, whose greatest
dream of change was being offered a job by someone

rich. To these people Brother Michel brought nothing but a willingness to listen—he had nothing else to bring— but it seemed to the people that peace rested for a moment around the hard wooden stool where he sat.

In Barreira das Almas it was soon apparent to Brother Michel that there was nothing for him to do. Father Gil's routine took him from the rectory to the church, where he said mass daily, twice on Sundays. At other times, people dribbled into the rectory for confession or for wedding and baptism preparations, which the old priest insisted on doing himself. An elderly cook took care of the meals and housework. Turning to what he knew, Brother Michel organized the numerous, miscellaneous books in the house into a little library, but what then?

He fell back on his habit of visiting the poor. He would go from one thatched adobe or wattle house to another, and would be welcomed as anyone would be welcomed, sitting in the shade of the house on a square stool as the people themselves sat, saying little and listening a lot— ten minutes, half an hour, an hour—then would stand up with the rituals of leave taking:

"But it's early, *Irmão* Michel."

"Yes, yes. It's always early when one leaves friends."

"Come back again, *Irmão*."

He would pass on to the next house. And at each place people would pour out stories—stories of their lives, their loves, their fights, the deaths of their children—stories that in Belgium you would hear only from a close friend in utter privacy—told openly in front of sitting neighbors and staring children, staring not at the speaker but at the strange squat figure of *Irmão* Michel.

"...then he started to beat me so I joined up with another man—he's the father of that little brown one over there—but he went off to Mato Grosso and never came back, so..."

"...well, when I met her she was twelve, working down at the cabaret, and I thought—'this one has a nice fanny'—so, after I'd had her a few times, she moved in, and there's nothing for an old man like me to complain of..."

"...but that third baby, from the time he was born, I said to my sister—didn't I, Fátima?—that one's an angel—and sure enough, he was eight months old—when was it, April? no, May, and he started wasting away and died..."

Slowly, out of the stories—the drunken husbands, the abandoned wives, the children eaten away by malnutrition—a pattern began to emerge.

"It didn't used to be like this, *Irmão*. There used to be *fartura*—abundance, plenty."

Then they would tell of a time—long ago?—not so long—when there were fruit trees—oranges, lemons, guavas, papayas, mangos—when crops of rice and corn grew tall in small fields, when sugar cane and squash and coffee and melons abounded.

"The old people—the old people are strong, *Irmão*, not like those youngsters who never eat."

"What happened?"

"The men came..."

"The men?"

The men came, out of the south, in jeeps and carrying (though the people did not see them at first) guns, men with documents that they waved in front of the people's eyes. This is our land, the men said. You're trespassers invading our land. Get off.

"How long had you been on the land?" Brother Michel asked.

Fifteen years, thirty years. Sometimes their father had settled it, sometimes their grandfather.

"Didn't you know your rights?"

Rights? Who had rights against men from the south with jeeps and guns?

"But if you were twenty years on the land, you owned it." Brother Michel had gone and looked this up. "Even ten years, in some cases. And if you've been on the land even a year and a day, you can't be taken off without a court hearing."

"Yes, *Irmão*." Shrugs. What are rights when the police, the judges are working for the men from the south with jeeps and guns? And with money.

"What did you do?"

At first the people hadn't known their rights; many accepted a tiny indemnification and left their land. Then a few of the farmers started to find out. One group of families hired a lawyer, but he was scared off. Houses burned, crops were destroyed. More people left the land. Those that remained were isolated, vulnerable. Threats, beatings. More people leaving. A few staying on. A killing. The others ran.

It happened, again and again, in new waves as each new area of land was taken. Two thousand, three thousand families pushed off their land.

"But there are still some small farms left."

Yes. A few areas. Eleven families at Córrego Branco, fifteen at Santa Maria, twenty-five at Santana, a couple of dozen at Agua Fria....

There was an old motorcycle in the garage, and the boy from the mechanic's shop was able to get it going. Brother Michel had never ridden a motorcycle, but he'd ridden bicycles and the idea was the same. He began riding, practicing, falling off and badly skinning one knee, but getting the hang of it after a while.

He visited Agua Fria first, riding out in the dust, a small boy perched behind him to teach the way. When he got there, he found a tumbled down adobe house swarming with children. The woman came out to meet him. The boy explained who he was. The man was in the fields they'd send for him. Brother Michel, sitting an hour on a hard wooden bench. The man coming in from the field, tired and sweating. "Tell me about yourself," Brother Michel said, and much later, "I'd like to talk to all of you. Can you find a day when your neighbors can come together?"

"Listen, Brother Michel," the Church lawyer said over the static telephone line from Conceição, two hundred miles away by rough dirt roads. "I can defend them in court. I can keep the judge from issuing an order to evict them. But only they can keep themselves on the land."

The single telephone in town was at the telephone office, a little plastered brick building on the main street, where people waited in line for the operator to put through their calls. Brother Michel looked around the small, crowded room. Every word he said into the telephone — nearly shouting, as everyone did — would, he knew, be heard by everyone in the room and repeated as rumor all over town.

"You mean?..." he asked the lawyer.

"I mean there are only two of us, and we cover an area the size of France. Not Belgium, France."

"I understand that."

"We can take care of the legal end, but most of the threats aren't legal. Gunmen, policemen hired to do this on the side, burnings..."

"Yes, I know..."

"If the people hold together, if they stick it out, we can win them their land. But usually they can't stick."

2

As he realized the weight of power against them, Brother Michel began to have a dream.

The weight was enormous. Documents issued by the state government, highly placed politicians with a stake in the land claims, corrupt judges and police, gunmen, a law that rarely punished a rich man for killing a poor one but crucified a poor man who resisted the rich.

A federal government that didn't care, that saw any resistance as a danger to be put down. An uninterested press that was too far away. A people unsure of themselves, scared, living—as they themselves put it— at the far edge of the world.

The dream—it was only a day dream—was that a hero would arise, somewhere, somehow, to save the people.

It took shape one evening when he was watching television on the wavy blurry transmission that came in sporadically when the usually broken parabolic antenna functioned for a few days. There was a melodrama on about 19th century Brazil, the time of the slaves, and that stock character stolen from old American and European films: a young nobleman, disguised in a mask and cape, sweeping out of the night to right wrongs, to avenge injustice. And Brother Michel began to dream.

"The best proof of ownership is the improvements they have on their land." The lawyer's voice sounded a thousand miles away over the telephone line. "Fruit trees, fences, houses, wells..."

The next day Brother Michel squatted on his haunches, like the three farmers with him, in a field in Córrego Branco. How can we get wire for fencing? Who can cut fence posts? When can we get everyone together to put up fences?

*   *   *

Sometimes the hero would ride into town at night, masked and swathed in his dark cape, mounted on a black horse. He would stop in front of the house of a landowner's agent and draw his sword. Leaning from the saddle, he would swiftly carve a warning sign on the door, while inside the agent sat paralyzed with fear. In the morning, the agent would come out of his house and tremble when he saw the sign....

"If they have a municipal school on the land, anywhere among the homesteads," the static-filtered lawyer's voice said, "it's harder for the landowners to evict them."

"The families at Santana have built a school," Brother Michel said to the municipal prefect a month later, picturing in his mind the wattle-walled, thatched roof classroom which the people had come together on three Saturdays to build. "They need you to assign them a teacher."

"But they're just *posseiros, Irmão*; they have no title to their land."

"What difference does that make? Where there are children there should be schools."

"True, *Irmão*, but..."

"And they have eighty-one voters out there. Imagine that. I counted them; eighty-one. A dozen of them are waiting outside to talk to you now..."

"I agree, *Irmão*, they need a school. But I have no teachers..."

"Oh, they've found someone who can be a teacher. If you'll just sign here to show that she can officially teach in the municipal system..."

"Well, *Irmão*..."

"I'll just call the families in now, so that they can see you..."

* * *

Sometimes the hero would be hard and lean-faced, smoking a cigarette and wearing a panama hat like a detective in an old French film. His car (in Brother Michel's vision it was always an old model Citroen, though such a car had never been seen on these roads) would pull into town as the landowners and gunmen were organizing, where Brother Michel and the *posseiros* stood alone. The car door would open and the hero would step out, a bulge where his shoulder holster rode under his tight beige suit jacket. And the landowners' gunmen would look up, afraid....

"They need to keep together, Brother Michel." The lawyer's voice on the telephone. "If they can keep together, they can hold out long enough for us to win the case."

Sunday afternoon at Santa Maria. The thirty-first Sunday meeting since Brother Michel first called them together, and the fifth since they built the small wattle-walled palm-thatched chapel. Sometimes he cannot be here, is off in one of the other areas, but he has helped them learn what to do. Today he is here, but the people carry on with their meeting as they do when he cannot come.

A farmer stands up and opens the Bible to the day's gospel reading. Slowly—in the voice of a man newly practiced in reading—he proclaims the passage, pauses, then reads it aloud again so that his listeners can absorb it. The passage speaks of vines and branches, of how fruit will not grow on a dead branch, a branch separated from the vine, from the soil. Things these people understand deeply and, looking at them, Brother Michel realizes once again that these are very much like the people Jesus was talking to. The language of farms, livestock, kitchens, and small towns, is their language. The reader sits down and the men and women begin to speak, bringing their lives to the words, sharing, intertwining.

Sometimes it was not a hero but a heroine. Drifting off to sleep, Brother Michel would see the *posseiros*, his *posseiros*, drawn together and a line of gunmen and police moving in to beat and burn. Suddenly, out of the rainforest, on a white horse, glistening in her armor, rides a woman, and all eyes turn to her but only he knows her, and his lips silently form the word, "Joan..."

The young policeman stood, hat in hand, large but bashful, like an overgrown boy, the young woman, pretty, dark-skinned, tiny beside him.

"We're supposed to be married tomorrow," the policeman said. "We came for the preparation. Father Gil is sick. He said that you..."

Me? Brother Michel had never prepared a couple for marriage in his life. He hesitated a moment, then reached deep down inside himself; he knew so many families, what they were going through. He knew the theology, the Bible passages, the teaching of the Church. He knew what it was to vow your life to something and stay with it through all kinds of disappointments. He searched through his mind to remember the policeman's name.

"Ivaldo..." Brother Michel began.

3

The first death threat came three months after he started visiting the *posseiros*. It was an innocuous looking note left at the telephone office, which served as the nerve center for rumors. "The little priest will die," the note said, which was inaccurate, as Brother Michel pointed out to the three townsmen who rushed to bring him the news. "I'm not a priest."

The three men were poor, men who had lost their land and now lived by fishing and planting rice on the floodlands and little islands that emerged from the river during the dry season. They looked at him with a mixture of puzzlement and concern: these fine ecclesiastical distinctions lay beyond their realm of interest.

"But the note was meant for you, *Irmão*," one of them said.

"Yes. I suppose it was."

It wasn't an empty threat, he knew. A priest had been murdered in the neighboring state a few months ago, another out west last year. Several sisters had been killed, a Baptist minister, a number of lawyers and union leaders, and many, many small farmers. But no brothers, he reflected wryly. Yet.

He went to bed that night and couldn't sleep, listening to the mosquitoes buzzing outside the mosquito net, his stomach in knots. The electricity, generated by a municipal diesel motor, was turned off at eleven p.m., so there was nothing much to do except lie there in the dark until three a.m., when he got up and stumbled to the bathroom where he sat on the toilet, his stomach cramped with diarrhea, waiting for the morning to come.

His fear—and he knew it was fear—was strange to him. The world is a dangerous place, and he had known general fears before—airplanes and heights and sudden panic when walking across the crazy traffic streets in Rio. But never before had he been the direct target of a threat—never had he felt that someone wanted him, specifically, Michel, to die.

And the fear was a funny one. He didn't think he was afraid of being dead. He had had his doubts as all

men do, but his faith was deep: he believed that he
would be with God in the afterlife. The fear he felt was
like when he had to fix an electric plug — that suddenly
220 volts of shock and pain would shoot through him.
He had always, he knew, been a timid man — wary of
bangs and bursts and making messes. He almost felt
guilty, a small boy playing with explosives that he wasn't
old enough to handle, afraid they'd go off and scare him,
hurt him, hurt someone else. He wished with all his heart
that someone strong would come who could carry this
burden, lift it from his shoulders, really help the people.

"Never travel alone," the lawyer's voice said. "Never
open your door until you know who's outside. Never..."
    But who had time to think of those things? He was
busy now, not only in the country but the town: burying
the dead, visiting the sick, helping Dona Angela with
the rosary group or the five teenagers who came to him
wanting to form a youth group. What time was there to
be thinking of fear?

Two months later, the second threat was nailed to the
Church door. "Brother Michel will die," it announced
in crudely printed letters. More accurate, he pointed out
to the women from the rosary group who brought it to
him, and really not a threat, only a statement of fact.
    It came as tensions were growing. Each year, during
Lent, the Church had a national campaign focusing on
a particular social problem, and this year it was land
reform. Father Gil had not been feeling well and
increasingly had been depending on Michel to assume
more pastoral tasks. About this time, the old priest asked
if Brother Michel would be willing to prepare and
deliver the homilies at mass; Father Gil would celebrate
but would sit in his chair by the altar resting while

Brother Michel—dressed in the gray habit, which he only wore for religious functions—spoke about the readings and the message they brought. Because of this, the people identified the Church's position on land reform with Brother Michel, thinking it was "the little priest" who was stirring up an issue that meant trouble.

In the days after the threat was nailed on the door, Brother Michel noted the people watching him whenever he walked through the streets. In this dull little decaying town, the threat created drama, a new source for rumors, and he sensed that the people—even those who wished him no harm—tingled with dreadful anticipation, waiting for something to happen. He even half suspected that the note had not been written by a landowner or a gunman, but by some bored townsperson desperately in need of excitement.

"You should have a jeep, not a motorcycle," the lawyer's voice recommended, "and always travel with half a dozen people. You need to be very careful..."

He was careful.

Diesel pick-up trucks and jeeps were the only viable transportation for the rough dirt roads, and they almost always belonged to landowners or their allies. He learned to be jumpy when he heard one coming. If he were out on his cycle and heard them in time, he would pull off and hide in the bush. But only if he were certain he would not be seen—he instinctively knew that it would be dangerous to let them see he was afraid. If he could not be certain of hiding, he would keep riding his cycle as the large vehicles swept by, intensely aware that they could swerve and run him off the road, maiming or killing him with the mere flick of their steering wheel.

He would be safer with a jeep, but how could he afford one? If the Order in Rio de Janeiro knew of the work he was doing, they might buy him a jeep; more probably, they would close down the mission and call him and Father Gil back to Rio, deeply concerned for their safety. After a few months, when the Church lawyer made a visit to Barreira, Brother Michel explained the problem and the lawyer spoke to the bishop about it. The bishop had to write to Germany, but a jeep would be coming, Brother Michel learned, in about six months. In the meantime, "Be very careful..." the lawyer's voice repeated.

The third threat was not a note but a drunken gunman in the Diablo Bar, announcing to all the world that he was going to get the little priest. A couple of farm workers heard him and came to the rectory. It was Sunday evening, just before mass.

"You shouldn't go to the church, tonight, *Irmão*," one of the farm workers said. He was a straightforward, intelligent man, about Michel's age, and he twisted his hat in his hand as he spoke. But, of course, Michel went to mass, small groups of women, old men, young people flocking around him as he walked the half block to the church.

"*Irmão* Michel, did you hear..."

The mass was more crowded than usual, with an air of expectation and an unusual number of men, so Michel preached about marital fidelity, which the Lord knew they needed to hear about, but was not the titillation they hoped for, and reflected wryly to himself on the value of death threats in increasing attendance at mass. "Go right home now," Dona Angela from the rosary group said kindly at the end of mass, but he stayed to talk, to listen, for a few minutes.

* * *

"Brother Michel."

Father Gil's voice called out from the sitting room as Michel entered the rectory, and Michel went into the room. The old priest had hobbled home right after mass, leaning on the arm of a young parishioner. He sat now in his big, wooden-armed, padded chair, his eyes bright behind glasses.

"Sit down, Michel."

Michel sat on the red vinyl couch and leaned back.

"They tell me there is a gunman who says he is going to kill you."

"He's drunk," Michel said, dismissing the matter.

"The most dangerous time," Father Gil answered. He paused for a moment, his face stern. "It is only now that I learned that there were some notes, some threats..."

"I didn't want to bother you about those..."

"Bother me! Am I *that* old that you can't tell me you are in danger?"

"They weren't really anything. Besides..." He stopped.

"Besides, we wouldn't want Rio to know." The old man completed Brother Michel's thought, then chuckled at the surprised expression that flitted across Michel's face.

"I know," Father Gil said softly. "I am old, and often it is convenient to pretend I do not know, but I know." He paused and Michel wondered for an instant what the old man was referring to. "They will close this place when I am dead."

It was a dry statement of fact, demanding no answer. The two men sat in silence for a moment.

"What you are doing is important, Michel." He smiled. "For my part—I will stay alive as long as I can. I wish I could do more, but that I can do. You do it too—take care of yourself."

Michel nodded. He was wishing in a blurred, exhausted way, that God would answer his dream, his prayer, and send a hero to help the *posseiros*.

That night, drifting off to sleep, thinking of the masked hero riding into town, his sweeping sword marking signs on the land agents' doors....

Signs on doors. The hero was no longer a masked man but a tall, strong, bearded Moses, a prince of the people who had seen God burning in the jungle bush. Signs not on doors but on door posts, not threatening but protecting the anawim, the little people. Dark clouds over the houses of the rich in distant cities—Belém, Goiania, Brasília, São Paulo—and Moses lifting up his strong arms: 'Let my people live on their land... Let my people live..."

4

Morning brought one of those comic denouements which so often strike when danger threatens. The drunken gunman, sallying out of the bar at midnight, swearing to kill Brother Michel, met a former cohort who had called him a son of a whore the week before, took a full force swing to punch him and, missing, slammed his fist into a pick-up truck, breaking his hand and wrist. By morning the threatener was holed up at a local ranch, his trigger hand bound in bandages and the danger, for the present, had passed.

But afternoon brings its own challenges, and it came in the form of a small boy running to tell Brother Michel that he was wanted at the telephone office. The call, the girl at the post said when he got there, had been from the lawyer, who would call back in half an hour.

"We've just learned that they got a court order to oust the families from Agua Fria," the lawyer's voice said over the line.

"But that's illegal," Brother Michel protested.

"Of course it is. We'll get it reversed in a few days. But in the meantime we can't let them take the people off the land. Once they're off the land, it's almost impossible to get it back.

"They'll move quickly, probably tomorrow at dawn. They're gathering police here, and will pick up a few there...

"The police will burn the crops and houses...

"Keep the people on the land."

The police did not make it by dawn. It was ten a.m., the sun high and hot, when the first truck in the convoy of seven vehicles rounded a bend in the dirt road to Agua Fria: seven drivers, three men in sports shirts and sunglasses, thirty men in police uniforms—half of them real policemen—and thirty more hangers-on with guns in their belts. The first truck slowed, then came to a halt, and one of the men in sunglasses, riding in the cab, swore under his breath. A hundred feet in front of them, barbed wire stretched across the road. Behind the barbed wire stood a hundred men, women, and children, and, this side of the barbed wire, three or four men, a dozen ladies holding rosary beads, a group of teenagers from town, and a damn little friar in a gray habit. Singing. All of them singing some damn church song. And the convoy motors turning off one by one, truck and jeep doors slamming, men climbing down from the trucks to look, the little man in the gray habit calling out to some of the police by name—"Good morning, Ivaldo; Good morning, Edivan," thick glasses catching the sunlight above a ridiculous squat figure with a silly foreign accent.

Three nights later, exhausted, Brother Michel falls into bed: two nights sleeping with the others by the fence—

even after the convoy had turned around that first morning and driven away, sleeping by the fence to be prepared, in case, until the message came from the telephone office in town. We beat them off this time. But this will go on and on, forever, and Dear God, how long can we hold out? Drifting and, suddenly, as he is half-asleep, dreaming the dream again: this time it is a strong figure, gleaming and translucent, walking boldly through the tall grass to stand beside them, facing the police, facing the gunmen.

And Brother Michel prays with his last waking thoughts as his head nestles into the pillow: Oh Lord, send a hero for your people.

Two Foxes

(Tocantins, 1991)

Foxes," Adão said.

It was six in the morning. October, a cool day at the beginning of the rainy season. The two foxes stood outlined against the gray morning sky on the dirt road ahead of us. Brazilian foxes: slightly larger than a North American fox, brownish gray, sturdy, with great bushy tails. I slowed the jeep. The lead fox darted ahead into the tall grass at the right side of the road. The other hesitated a moment, then turned and vanished off to the left.

"Foxes," he said again. His big black face peered across me into the bush on the left, to see if he could spot the one that had run there. Then a deep, loving laugh rolled out from his big body.

"You have many of them out at your farm?" I asked.

"Quite a few."

"They go after the chickens?"

"They sure do."

The jeep bumped along another half mile. I thought of that deep, rolling laugh. It was not the usual response to foxes.

"Most of the time, when there's someone in the car with me and we see a fox, they tell me to run it down." I shifted into second and maneuvered around a mud hole. "I never do, though."

We rode along in silence for a while. I glanced over at him—his gray hair and mustache, his big work-hardened hands, the new blue shirt and recently pressed gray pants he had worn into town.

"They almost always travel in couples like that, don't they?" I asked.

He smiled—a big, slow smile.

"I was just thinking of that," he said. "It reminded me of something that happened a few years ago."

"What was that?"

Adão didn't answer right away. I was thinking of his farm, where we were now headed. How you come to it over a slight rise. It lies in a green valley, looking like a farmstead might have looked any time in the last hundred years—the adobe house and outbuildings with palm-leaf thatched roofs, the wooden split-rail fences. He lives there with his daughter, his son-in-law, and their three children.

"It was a year or so after Adela died," he said. Adela was his wife. "A couple of hours before dawn. I was lying in my hammock, awake—staring at the dark, not wanting to get up and stir around so as not to wake the others. Suddenly I heard barking and growling—almost like a dog fight. I rolled out of the hammock, put on my boots, grabbed my flashlight and rifle, and headed out the door.

"It was a moonlit night. We had three dogs then, and I saw them over by the fence. They had something cornered. We'd been having trouble with foxes—so I guessed that's what it was. You know—when you farm like we do, you don't have much. Losing chickens hurts—and I was mad as hell. I raised my rifle and called off the dogs so that I could get a clear shot. The dogs backed off—I shot and saw the fox leap up once and fall. I walked over—it was a big male, and he was dead—shot clean through the body. I started to turn back toward the house.

"Suddenly I glimpsed a rapid shadow scurrying from the end of the fence toward the woods. I wheeled, raised my rifle and shot. I heard a yip—but she kept running. It was a she-fox I was sure—smaller than the dead male. I fired again, but she was already into the woods and gone.

"The dogs went wild and started to chase her—but I called them off and walked toward the house. Everybody was awake now, of course, the grandkids rolling wide-eyed out the door wanting to see what had happened. So we took care of the dead fox, and talked, and my son-in-law and I told the kids all the fox stories we knew—and then some—and my daughter made us all a big breakfast. And that was that."

He went into one of his long pauses as I downshifted and headed up a winding, rutted slope. I waited.

"Except, well... I couldn't get it out of my mind. It kept eating at me. So, along about mid-morning, I took my rifle and the oldest dog, and I started out toward the woods.

"I'd hit her, all right. It was easy enough to see that. There was blood where I'd hit her, and blood here and there on the brush along the trail. That old dog and I had done our share of tracking, and it was easy enough to follow where she went. We curved off way to the southeast, until we came to a place where she seemed to have settled down for a while. Then the trail headed straight north.

"Now I'm no expert on foxes—or on anything else, for that matter—but there was only one reason I could think of for her doing that. As it turned out, I was right.

"Well, we headed north along her trail. The dog I brought with me was an old fellow—old enough to have some sense." He smiled at me. "Dogs are a lot like people in that way. Anyhow, he knew how to go quietly and not get over excited, and keep his nose down and do his work. More than you can say for some folks."

He chuckled—a deep sound from down inside—then sat quietly a few seconds before continuing.

"When you've been in and out of the woods as long as I have, you get a sense for things. We reached a spot where I had that sense. I told the dog to lie down and be still. I moved forward, silently—slowly, pausing every few seconds. It wasn't close—it took me maybe half an hour to go a hundred yards. There was a small rock hill in front of me, with a cover of bush. Her trail— dim but still visible—led up to it. I moved slowly, quietly, raised my rifle with my right arm and pushed the branches aside quickly with my left.

"There she was. Not ten feet away—her teeth bared and her eyes on my eyes. My bullet that morning had hit her right shoulder—grazed deeply. The wound was still open, bleeding a little. She had lost blood—probably lost some mobility—and was tired. But that's not why she didn't run from me now. Behind her were three pups."

We had reached the final turn off to his farm. I slowed the jeep to navigate the narrower road.

"I want to explain how it was," he said. "A man has a right to defend what is his. A man has to feed his family—to fight off anything that steals from the mouths of his grandchildren. A man has a right to kill a fox."

He was silent for a moment.

"But a man also has a right—sometimes—not to kill."

We came over the last rise. The farm lay below us, beautiful and peaceful in the morning light.

"Here we are—home!" His voice was filled with contentment.

"Wait a minute!" I said, as I steered the jeep down the final slope. "What happened? What did you do?"

"What do you think I did?" he asked, laughing heartily.

"And you still have trouble with foxes?"

"Sure do. Probably the pups I left her to raise. That's gratitude for you, huh?" And he smiled.

Four Liters of Wild Honey

(Tocantins, 1991)

S hatter. Crack.

João heard the bottle shatter an instant before the gunshot. Heard it and felt it. In his own slow way, he looked up to where the four clear-glass bottles of honey had stood, on a wooden railing, golden in the sunlight. Stood where they caught sunlight and the eyes of drivers on the Belém-Brasília highway—drivers who might stop and buy at his sister Marilda's roadside stand.

Shatter. Crack.

Another bottle shattered to the ground, bleeding gold honey into the roadside gravel. João's slow middle-aged body started forward with uncharacteristic speed, his mind focused on saving the remaining two bottles. But even as he got there—shatter, crack—he felt the swish of the bullet and a third bottle shattered to the ground. He grabbed the fourth and pulled it close to his body— a slow motion goalie retrieving a rebound.

"*Idiota!*"

He turned and looked at the pick-up truck, at the big florid man leaning on the open passenger door, pistol in hand. It was a new shining-white, double-cabined truck with a chrome, shark-toothed grill—bright even despite road dust. The truck was perhaps fifty feet away, pulled up at the other end of the stand. Beyond it, the empty two-lane highway stretched north across the dry, flat savannah land.

Marilda was standing a few feet away with the driver of the pickup – a smaller, darker man who was drawing bills out of his wallet to pay for fresh corn. They both froze for a moment, staring at the big man with the pistol. Then they moved quickly.

"What is this?" Marilda shouted angrily as the driver started toward the truck, toward the man with the pistol. "Luís!" the driver shouted.

The big florid man turned to him.

"Tell that idiot to get out of the way," he complained. He was drunk. The driver reached him, spoke to him quietly, urgently. Luís seemed to lose interest, allowing the driver to take the pistol out of his hand and coax him back into the truck.

"What is this?" Marilda shouted again, her sharp voice piercing the air.

The driver turned back to her. "I'm sorry, my brother…"

"That's wild honey," she said. "Fifteen *cruzados*…" João looked up startled. Normally they sold them for nine.

"…and we have to clean up this mess."

Embarrassed, the driver was reaching in his wallet, pulling out a fifty note, then another twenty. "Here," he said. And then again, confused, "I'm sorry…"

He picked up his sack of corn, put it in the back of the truck, walked around to the driver's door and got in. The door banged shut—strong metal—the engine revved up, the truck pulled out into the highway and headed south toward Goiania.

João eased down onto his three legged leather stool. He was still holding the fourth bottle. Marilda walked over to him. She was counting the money.

"You all right?" she asked.

He slowly nodded.

She was quiet for a moment, looking at the three shattered bottles, the gold honey—bright with splintered glass—flowing out onto the gravel.

"We made a lot more than we would have," she said.

He nodded again.

He sat on his three legged stool. He could sit there for hours—watching, thinking. "Let me handle the money," Marilda had always said. He knew how to count it, how to make change. But she was right—it didn't mean anything to him.

He looked again at the shattered bottles, lying on the ground. Did *she* understand? Going out beyond the field, into the savannah backland—the wind-twisted trees, the low growing ground palms, the endless grass. You saw the bees and followed them, finding the hive. You gathered dried leaves and twigs and *lenha*—small limbs of dry, twisted wood. Carefully you placed them, preparing them with knowing hands. You had to do it just right to make smoke, enough smoke. You lit the fire, then walked away and stood back, watching— watching the smoke slowly rise and grow thicker, the bees begin to leave the hive—then their movement, a few at first going off and suddenly the whole swarm rising and flying away.

Then the hive itself. The careful handling of the rich white-yellow honey combs. Later, at home, filtering the golden liquid into the clear bottles. Thinking (with pictures, not with words)—this will bring memory to the lips of old people, now living in the city—memory of the countryside where they were young; this will bring happiness to children—eating quickly and licking with swift tongues; this will bring sweetness to men and women who rush, burdened, through their days.

His eyes caressed the shattered bottles, the shards of glass, the gold flowing into the ground. Slowly he rose and walked over to the wooden railing, and placed the last remaining bottle where it caught the bright afternoon sun.

A big Mercedes truck whirred by, raising a brief breeze. The noise of its motor grew fainter and fainter as it moved north. The silence of the savannah remained. Off to the west he heard the cry of the timid ground bird—*inhambu chororó*—calling out its notes in a descending scale.

THE MOVING
(Espírito Santo, 1969)

It was a day like any day. Maria put wood onto the fire in the brick stove. She looked at the water she had set in the pot to heat, then out the kitchen door to where the baby sat, bare-bottomed on the dry ground, and pleased himself by picking up fistfuls of dust and flinging them aimlessly. She would go now and sweep out the front room and the small tile-floored porch. Then she would come back and wash the baby.

She washed the baby every day since the woman who worked with the farm advisors told her there was less chance of him dying if he were washed. Maria's friend Penha was skeptical. But Maria had seen her first baby die—a small, weak creature who coughed and cried. If she could keep her babies from dying, she would do it.

It was a day like any day, except that in another day they'd be moving. One afternoon a few weeks earlier Zé had come in, sweating and tired after herding cattle, and said that Geraldo, the manager, had told him Senhor Carlos had sold the *fazenda* to a man from Vitória who would be moving in his own herd and his own men. Zé and Maria and the other three families who worked the *fazenda* would have to leave.

Senhor Carlos was rich, but not unkind. He drove out from the city in his jeep to take care of some business, and promised his workers he would find them places to go. He had done so. Two of the families had already left. Only Maria's family and Penha's remained.

She finished sweeping the porch and looked up. In front of the house was a wide grassy area, big enough to hold cattle, around which—almost at the corners—stood the four workers' houses. They were small, but built of brick covered neatly with plaster, with red tile roofs and red ceramic tile floors. A few hundred meters to the south was the big house—closed now as it usually was—a single story surrounded by a large verandah. Beyond, the land spread flat under the light blue sky, south past the dirt road and into the forest, and east across pastures as far as she could see.

She turned and walked inside. She would miss this house. The house where she had grown up had been made of wattle—mud and sticks—plastered over in parts where the plaster hadn't worn through. Its floor had been dirt, pressed hard enough so that you could sweep it almost clean, but turning muddy when rain leaked through the old tile roof. In this house, when water leaked through the tiles in the hard rains, it could be swept off the floor. And here there was a pump in the kitchen; she didn't have to walk to the river for water.

Returning to the kitchen, she found the water too warm. She set a huge metal basin on the table and poured the water into it to let it cool.

Watching the water, clean and clear in the metal basin, she was caught up in thoughts as still as a clear forest pool. Her thoughts were of green and gentle things: her grandfather holding her hand as they walked through a pasture, then lifting her high and looking at her with gentle brown eyes; Epifânia, her sister, laughing, with thrown grass in her hair; her brother poling a canoe across the green forest river. These images quieted her and made her feel deep, and for a minute she rested in them.

Then there was another thought, not still but exciting, even after five years: the clear black eyes of Zé the night she knew she loved him and he stood, holding both her hands and looking into her eyes, at the dance on São João's day. The priest had been there; there was a mass, and after mass a *festa* with food and dancing and Zé holding her hands and looking deeply into her eyes with his eyes, clear and unbelievably black.

The prayers before mass: she remembered, ever since she was a little girl, the Ave Marias rising and falling, a warm flood of sound, constant. When she was very little, she understood only the first words of it—"Ave Maria, cheia de graça"—and all the rest was just warm and comforting sound until the next "Ave Maria, cheia de graça." Even when she was older and knew the words by heart, she liked to pretend she didn't and just hear the "Ave Maria, cheia de graça" and then the gentle rise and fall of sound.

That night the men had sat and drunk *cachaça* and talked of the crops and the weather, and some of the men who had lived there all their lives talked of the old days. Then talk turned to the world: to the new road and Linhares. Men who had been born elsewhere told stories of Bahia and Montanha and Nanuque, and they spoke of Vitória and of São Paulo, where it was said any young man could find a job.

Zé talked with them, now also accepted as a man, having gone out and worked and returned with a job and money. He spoke of the *fazenda* near Linhares, of the cattle, of riding the tough young horses and mules. The men listened to him almost with respect, though now and again chiding him with being young and eager, telling him it was time to find a wife; and the men who had known cattle up in Montanha listened and nodded and agreed with what he said. Slightly outside the group, the women and girls listened; Maria pressed closely to Epifânia's side, watching Zé, and she thrilled every time he turned and looked into her eyes.

A year later they were married, and within a year after that the baby was born. But before the baby came, they left the region where she had grown up and came here, to the place where Zé was working—where he herded cattle and rode the small hard cattle horses across the grassland. They'd come down the narrow dirt roads, she and Zé and her little sister, Estrela, riding in the open back of a truck with a few belongings piled around them, riding ninety kilometers from her father's wattle house, ninety kilometers to a different world, Zé happy in the sunlight that shone through the trees, putting his arm around her.

The first child died, but before another year passed, their second was born: a strong happy son called José after his father. Zé was proud of that son—talking to him now as a baby, now as a man—telling him he would raise him to herd cattle. It made her proud to see Zé so proud. And then, just a year ago, the third child had been born.

She looked out the back door and saw Estrela coming across the pasture with little Zé, the sun striking her light-colored hair. She came slowly, now carrying the child, now letting him walk a few paces at her side, now playing with him, half noticing him, half alone in her own thoughts.

Estrela was Maria's sister, though only eleven and just coming out of being a child herself. When Zé and

Maria came to live here, her mother said, "Take Estrela with you," because there were too many people at home, and she knew their house would be comfortable. Zé had thought a moment, then nodded silently; so Estrela had come with them.

Sometimes on Sundays Estrela and Zé would sit on the grass in front of the house, little Zé running between them while the baby sat on the ground not far away and watched. Maria, on the porch, her hands absorbed in sorting black beans, would half watch the child running back and forth. Then she would smile and, glancing up from her hand work, would see Zé watching her and, underneath the talk and laughter, smiling at her, especially, warmth for her in his dark, black eyes.

She called out, "Estrela!" and Estrela came across the grass, stooping through the wire fence and carefully guiding the child through after her. Leaving the child just inside the fence, she came up to the house, barefoot and brown. Watching her, Maria thought of Epifânia, the sister she'd grown up with, dark and bright eyed and laughing. Maria thought how much Estrela looked like Epifânia: the shape of her face, the laughter in her eyes. Yet she was not so dark; her hair was not deep black, her laughing eyes were light and not deep brown, and her skin was the browned skin of a blonde, not the brown skin of Epifânia.

Maria stooped and picked up the baby, then told Estrela there were things to do: beans to clean, and rice, and the chickens to be looked after. Estrela set about her work.

It pleased Maria to have Estrela work with her, for often Estrela would laugh and sing and chatter a young girl's chatter, making Maria smile to be with her. Other times

Estrela would be quiet and thoughtful, and then Maria also could think her own thoughts. But today Estrela was talking, her hands working through the beans separately from her thoughts.

"When will Zé be back?"

"I don't know."

"Do you think he'll see the new house?"

"Yes."

"What will the house be like?"

"I don't know, *querida*."

"As nice as this one?"

"If God wishes."

"It will probably be more like our house. Papa's, I mean." She sounded like a woman and then suddenly again like a child: "Won't it?"

"I don't know."

They fell silent, each thinking, each one's hands working separately from her thoughts.

Through the front door she saw Zé coming across the grass. The bright sun shone on his small leather hat and his dusty clothes. Beneath the hat his hair was dark and curly, his face brown.

He stepped onto the porch and walked across it. His boots clicked on the tile, and he took off his hat as he walked. In three strides he was in the door; he stopped, reached out and dropped the hat on the table. He was looking at her, his brown cheeks thin and unshaven, his eyes deep black and brilliant. She waited for him to speak, as she always waited.

"I've been to see the new place," he said.

"Yes."

"It's not as good as this place. It's wooden. But it will do. It's a little bigger. There's no pump in the kitchen."

He paused.

"I won't be working with cattle. I'll be working with cacau and bananas, and in the curing shed."

She didn't speak. She thought of him on the small cattle pony, riding hard and lean and brown, and she knew he felt free and happy herding cattle. At night he would come in hot and tired and strong and would take off his leather hat and hold it in his hand as he lifted back his head and laughed, showing his teeth, his black curly hair wild and free.

She knew how the work would be: the cacau, the bananas, the curing shed. Slow crops, low and hot by the riverside, and the sun beating down on the metal roof of the curing shed, the roof that slid back on wheels to let the sun beat on the cocoa beans and on the endless sweating backs of the men turning the cocoa beans.

Zé reached out his hand and laid it along the side of her face, his fingers touching her hair, his palm on her cheek. She was quiet.

Before dawn, as the sky turned slowly from black to gray, from gray to pale yellow, Maria, walking out from the kitchen door, saw a horseman far out in the grasslands behind the houses. As she watched she knew it to be Tônio, Penha's husband, so much like Zé yet older and more silent, riding slowly and in the direction of the houses, as though he had been riding all night.

So much like Zé, lean and hard, yet older. He had been here when Zé had arrived—little more than a boy—and had seen Zé learn and grow to the ways of herding cattle. He was a silent man. Though he would sometimes talk with Zé and though Maria knew his wife Penha well, she knew little of him.

Now, as she watched, the horse came to a stop. Tônio stood up in the saddle and scanned the flat land in the growing light. Then, seeing Maria and knowing he was watched, he dropped back into the saddle without a sign to her and nudged the horse towards home.

They arrived with the truck in the afternoon—a medium-sized truck with a cab and an uncovered back. It stopped on the grass in front of the house, and Maria saw and mostly heard the driver descending from the far side of the cab while a young boy, perhaps seventeen, dark-haired but light-skinned and thin, got out on the side near the house. He dropped to the ground and smiled at her—a quick, friendly smile like a brother's— as the driver came around the front of the truck, stocky and broad chested, unshaven for three days, the top two buttons of his tan work shirt unbottoned, sweat patches under his arms. The driver looked to her standing alone on the porch, and she looked toward Zé, who was coming from the other house where he had been talking with Tônio. The driver looked that way too. Zé walked to them across the grass. The driver watched him, then turned his head, grated his throat and spat into the grass, then turned back again to watch Zé coming. When Zé was close enough, the driver said, "We're here to help you move the stuff." Zé nodded and shook the driver's hand and the boy's.

The boy's name, she learned, was Vincinho. When he saw her or Zé he smiled, and sometimes she heard him laugh as he lifted things to carry them to the truck, working with Zé, who was serious, and the silent driver. When she reached down to lift something heavy he would be there, pushing her aside and saying, "No, no"—lifting it himself to carry it out to the truck. Once she took the baby in her arms, and he stopped and talked to it and touched his finger to its nose and smiled at her before he went on with the lifting and loading.

Estrela came in from the fields behind the house and stood watching the men load the truck. Maria told her to help and asked her where she had been, trying to get her to chatter. But Estrela just smiled and leaned against the wall, one bare foot pressed against the plaster, very quiet, as though she didn't know what was happening.

The truck was loaded, its open bed filled with their furniture, boxes, the chickens, a dog. The driver wiped his hands on his trousers and, turning to Zé, asked, "Is there anything else?"

"Nothing."

"Then let's go." He moved around toward the other side of the truck. "You ride on back. There's room for the woman and the kids with us in front."

On the other side the driver's door clanged open, and he climbed in. Vincinho lifted little Zé up into the near side of the cab, then climbed in himself. He held his arms out so that Maria could hand him up the baby. "Come on," he said kindly. The driver was settling himself in his seat; his door clanged shut.

"Estrela can hold the baby," Maria said. "I'll ride in back."

The driver shifted the gear to neutral and started the motor. "There's room for you and the kids in front," he said.

Estrela climbed into the cab, and Maria lifted the baby up and put it into her arms, cradled onto her lap. Zé came up beside Maria. "There's room for you on the seat," he said. "Why don't you ride here in front?"

She turned and looked at him. "I'll ride with you in the back," she said.

He looked into her eyes. "All right," he said.

The night truck cast its own shadow. It moved along the dirt road rapidly, its lights picking out banana trees from the mass of forest on each side.

Riding on the back of the truck, sitting on the side of

their turned-over wardrobe, Maria was above the lights and could look into the depths of forest behind the trees that lined the road, depths unbelievably black where an occasional huge firefly would light itself an instant. Above her were the tops of the taller trees, themselves very black, even against the night sky.

The wind at her back, made by the movement of the truck, was cold, and she pulled her shawl close around her shoulders, but it didn't help. She sat and shivered a little, and braced herself against the bouncing of the truck and listened to the wheels rolling over the dirt and small stones—now faster, now slower, yet constant.

—*Ave Maria, cheia de graça*—and then the rise and fall of sound.

—*Ave Maria, cheia de graça*—and then the rise and fall of sound.

She looked toward the side of the truck where Zé was sitting, balanced on the side rail, among the chickens and the boxes and the furniture. The noise of the truck made it too difficult to speak.

She watched him take out a cigarette and put it to his mouth, and he lit a match which suddenly made a small hearth of the cup of his hands and threw warm firelight on his face. And Maria felt herself near that hearth and warmed by it, while all the world outside the hearth and his warmed face and her warmed heart turned darker and colder.

FAMINE

(The Brazilian Northeast, c. 1970)

S on of a whore!"

The driver slammed his fist down on the steering wheel of the stalled truck. The boy on the seat beside him looked up, frightened by his anger, frightened by the fear he sensed lurking beneath the anger. He watched the driver with wide-opened eyes.

"Son of a whore," the driver repeated, but this time quietly, intensely. He turned and looked out the window, and the boy looked too, out over the flat, barren land, still visible in the twilight, empty to the distant hills except for half-starved scrub trees. Empty, but—the boy knew—not empty.

"What are we going to do?" the boy asked. It was awhile since the sun had set behind the distant hills, and it was quickly growing dark. The lone paved highway stretched straight north in front of them, south behind them, its two lanes also empty.

"Do?"

The word galvanized the driver into action. He reached under the seat and brought out a flashlight, a wrench, and a short iron bar. He pushed the door part way open, paused a moment, then reached across the cabin and opened the glove compartment. He took out the revolver and put it in the boy's hands.

"Hold this," the driver said. Then he pushed against the door and swung to the ground. For an instant the boy saw him standing there in the dusk, knees bent, his lithe body ready to fight, the iron bar clutched in his fist like a club. Then he slammed the door and moved quickly around to the front of the truck, opening its snub-nosed hood.

The boy sat holding the gun, huge and heavy and awkward in his hands. He was sweating. The windows were closed against thick masses of tiny buzzing insects, but a few had gotten in anyway and they hovered around his eyes and ears with thin, irritating whining. The rain had started just three days ago, he knew—after how long?—bringing with it night heat and bugs and dark skies that closed out moon and stars. But not bringing food. Not yet.

And that was what they were carrying—food. In the shiny aluminum square back of the truck, inside the rear doors, doors padlocked against thieves and marauders, it lay stacked in boxes. Boxes of food for the black markets in the northeast, the drought land, where people were willing to pay twice, three times the prices in São Paulo. Their fortune.

But the truck had broken down. He could hear the wrench moving under the hood, searching futilely, a lost metallic ringing. Then the driver's hand appeared over the edge of the hood and slammed it shut, and the driver, looking once behind him warily, came back and opened his door and swung up into his seat. A swarm of insects followed him into the cabin.

"What is it?" the boy asked.

The driver threw the wrench and iron pipe on the floor and muttered something. "Fuel line," the boy thought it was, but it didn't matter. Whatever it was, they wouldn't be able to fix it. The boy sat, still holding the gun in his sweating hands, drops of sweat running down inside his shirt, his forehead and neck drenched, the insects angry in his eyes, his ears.

The driver moved. The boy looked up and saw two specks of light—headlights—far ahead. "Thank God," the driver said, and he felt along the seat, picking up the flashlight. He swung his door open again and jumped down onto the road, turning on the flashlight and waving it, came back to the cabin, reached in and blinked the truck's headlights twice, then was back out on the road, dancing around, flashlight in hand. The open door let slightly cooler air in, and the boy gave up fighting the insects and rolled down his window, feeling almost cool in his sweat, feeling better. The headlights were drawing close now; the driver waved the flashlight again. The headlights came on fast, then passed in a flash, and the boy saw it was a truck, a blue-bodied snub-nosed Mercedes truck just like their own. And then it was gone, and they heard the dying whine of the other truck's engine as it sped south.

They saw the first figure just after eleven o'clock.

It flitted off to their left, a thin darkness against the darkness, and the boy probably wouldn't have noticed it at all except that the driver suddenly tensed and the boy looked where he was looking. A quick flitting, then it was gone.

"Give me the gun," the driver said.

The boy handed it to him, glad to be rid of the dead, heavy weight.

"Close your window," the driver said.

The boy closed it most of the way. The insects had died down, but the night was humid, hot. He left it open a few inches at the top.

"Is your door locked?" the driver asked.

The boy tested the knob with his fingers. "Yes," he said.

They sat in silence for a minute, and then the boy thought he saw another figure off to the right, then another. Circling. Closing in tighter.

The driver moved his hand slowly to the headlight knob. Suddenly he switched on the headlights. Three figures slipped aside quickly, out of the lights, vanishing like spirits, and the boy could only see that they were sticks of men—men or women—all bones, like a child's drawing. But they were gone, as though the light scared them away. The driver left the headlights on a minute or so—they could leave them on until the battery went dead, the boy knew, but what would they do then? The driver switched off the lights.

And again, after a few moments, the figures flitted across the edge of their sight. Again the driver flashed on the headlights, but this time he didn't catch any of the figures in the light. A faint, eerie laugh sounded off to their left.

They heard the first voice about a half hour later, off to the left, the driver's side, close by.

"Brother," the voice said quietly. "Brother, throw us out the key." A thin, rasping voice. "You and your truck won't be harmed."

Silence. The driver said nothing, but the boy could hear him breathing, breathing.

"Brother," another voice said. It was a woman's voice, whining and high. "Brother, we only want the food. We've eaten nothing for days. Have compassion, brother. Throw us the key."

"We all have pistols," the driver shouted, as though the cabin held three or four armed men, though there were only the two of them, and one gun.

Silence. A rattling on the outside of the truck as someone touched the running board, the door. First on one side, then the other.

"I'll shoot," the driver shouted.

Silence.

The boy screamed. A thin hand had reached through the partly closed window, grabbing his hair. In a panic he rolled the window shut, felt it close on the arm. A grunt of pain outside, and then the arm disappeared. He rolled the window up the rest of the way, his stomach turning over inside him.

"I'll shoot," the driver shouted more loudly.

Silence.

"Would you shoot an old woman, brother?" The driver jumped—the voice was just outside his door. "Don't you have a mother? Would you shoot an old woman?"

As if answering he half opened the window and, aiming wildly, high, shot into the night.

Silence.

The sound came a minute later. Metal against metal.

"They're prying at the back," the boy said.

The driver said nothing. The boy could feel his tenseness.

The sound came again, metal against metal, a crow bar, the boy thought, levered against the lock. Then a loud banging. Then the crow bar again.

The driver half turned, holding the gun high.

"Let them be," the boy said.

There was tense silence.

"Everything we have is back there," the driver said. He spoke quietly, intensely. "Everything we own."

"They can't break the lock," the boy said.

The sound of banging.

"Yes they can," the driver said. He pressed the keys into the boy's hand, flung open the door and leaped to the ground, clutching the gun. The door slammed shut.

The sound of metal stopped. The boy waited. Suddenly a shot barked out—once, twice. The sound of something soft hitting the back of the truck, soft pounding. A third shot.

The boy sweated in the closed cabin, trembling, his fingers hurting and tight around the keys. Slowly, as he listened, the sound of metal against metal started again.

GILSA
(Rio de Janeiro, 1979)

1

No one understood why Ademar married Gilsa. Or, as his brother-in-law said with a half smile, why he *married* her.

"He's too honorable," Ademar's sister answered. That was the afternoon following the wedding, and she thought Gilsa was pregnant. She was wrong, but she knew her brother very well.

Nelson Braga was a king in the slum called Morro Vermelho, two thousand shacks running up a hill in São Gonçalo, across the bay from Rio de Janeiro. On Saturday night he ruled at the samba school—Irmãos do Morro Velho—where all night long in weekly Carnaval the sweating dancers samba'd and the drums beat into the hot hill.

By day he stalked the dirt paths of the slum like a jaguar. Wherever he went, women were available. When he was sixteen, he got three thirteen-year-old girls pregnant. His father beat him and told Nelson he was too young to get married. He never did. He lived with one of the girls—as

much as he lived anyplace—a plain girl named Eva. She
bore six of his children; three of them died. He gave her
money for food. "If she wants anything else, she can earn
it," he said. He gave his other children nothing.

When Gilsa was eleven, Nelson started to notice her. He
was nineteen then. He would wander by her father's house,
stop at the bodega across the path and drink *cachaça*. His
shirt unbuttoned to the waist, he would lean against the bar
and talk with men about things that made him important.
All the time his eyes would watch Gilsa's young, lithe body.

If she happened to glance at him, her eyes would be
absolutely indifferent.

Gilsa never lied to Ademar about who she was. It wouldn't
have done any good. He could tell by her dark color, her
delicately scarred legs, that she was poor. She had gone to
the beach with her cousins, Juceléia and Nádia, and
Ademar, who was in from Rio Bonito visiting friends, had
seen her there. His friends, white, wealthy, like Ademar
himself, wandered over to talk to the girls. Juceléia, light
chocolate brown, was prettier than Gilsa, and Nádia, fiery-
eyed and defiant, was more dynamic. But it was Gilsa, self-
contained and animal tense, whom Ademar saw.

On the way back to Rio Bonito, Ademar drove the
girls home. It was out of his way. He parked the car at
the bottom of the hill and walked with them up the steep
path, stepping over mud and garbage, over sewage
streams. People stared at the sturdy, sandy-haired,
almost diffident stranger, walking up the hill, speaking
quietly now and then. At her father's house, he asked
Gilsa if he could come to see her again. She looked at
him for several seconds, then nodded.

Once when Gilsa was sixteen, Nelson Braga stopped
her on the path going down the hill. He was twenty-

four then, handsome, light brown, graceful. She was alone, and he laid his hand on her arm. She didn't move away. He said, "Come to the samba school tonight." He looked in her eyes and they were indifferent. He said in a soft, tight whisper, "Woman, you and I could be king and queen."

She brushed his hand aside and continued down the path.

It would have surprised Ademar's sister, who had a good deal of insight, to know that Gilsa was a virgin when she married. Not a virgin like her cousin Juceléia, who was saintly innocent and lighted up people's lives, or like Nádia, who wanted to go to law school and hated men. But a virgin in a tight self-held way, like an animal fighting for survival.

At the wedding, Ademar's sister was not embarrassed. She was genuinely gracious to Gilsa's family dressed in cheap finery and ill at ease. The shocked gossip that had greeted the announcement of Ademar's engagement had not touched her. The position of her family in Rio Bonito, she knew, was such that they made social styles rather than following them.

Nonetheless, she was not happy about Gilsa. It was not that Gilsa was poor. That cousin, Juceléia—Ademar's sister found her charming. Why couldn't he have chosen that one? She noticed the girl's dark eyes watching Ademar. Then Ademar's sister looked at Gilsa, and she thought of jungles.

The three girls were in the small front room of the shack where they lived with Gilsa's father. Ademar was coming that night: it was his third visit, long before any talk of engagement. Juceléia stood brushing Gilsa's hair as Gilsa looked at herself in the small mirror. Nádia sat studying on the bed that doubled as a couch.

"Well, I think he's nice," Juceléia said as she stroked with the brush. "Don't you, Nádia?"

Nádia didn't look up from her book. "You can't expect much from men." But she spoke half-heartedly. Even Nádia thought Ademar was pretty decent.

2

Gilsa moved through the rich house like an animal in a cage. It was hers, the smooth wood furniture, leather sofa, brocade curtains—all utterly strange.

At night, Ademar, home from work, would talk to her quietly over dinner, telling her about his day. Later, in bed, he would make love to her. He was very gentle. It was strange to her, something she did not understand, any more than she understood why Ademar's firm valued and paid him so highly, why people deferred to his quiet opinions.

They went back to Morro Vermelho nearly every weekend. Ademar was not irritated by this. He found himself looking forward to the weekends, felt strangely in touch with something he had never known before, strangely proud to walk up the hill no longer a stranger but greeted by name.

It was an hour's drive from Rio Bonito to Morro Vermelho, and often they would go and return the same day. The first time they spent Saturday night at his father-in-law's house, Ademar felt unaccountably happy, an initiate. His father-in-law gave them the back room. The double bed was narrow, the straw mattress scratchy and hard. Ademar slept badly but, at dawn, standing looking out the window while Gilsa and most of the slum slept, he felt newly alive.

Ademar's father-in-law was a thin old man, nut brown and without much personality. Quite early

Ademar had offered to help his father-in-law move out of the slum. The old man thought about it, his face blank, then shook his head. He'd lived on the hill twenty years. He let Ademar fix up the house, put in a bathroom, a new roof. And on the front of the house, where it sloped down the hill, he built a narrow wooden front porch.

The first time Gilsa went back to Morro Vermelho alone, Ademar was not upset. When he came home from work, she was gone. The maid told him where Gilsa was, that she would be back the next day. The maid, who had been with them three weeks, did not like Gilsa, and her face when she spoke was like light brown stone. Ademar sat down at the dinner table and ate alone.

A week later, Gilsa went again, and again spent the night. When she came back she didn't say anything, going on as before. Ademar could sense her restlessness, her watching him with dark eyes. Not hostile eyes, or frightened, but wary like a wild animal's. He tried speaking with her. At night her lovely wiry body tensed like an animal about to run.

Two weeks later, she didn't come home on the second day. Ademar, arriving from work, found only the maid at home. It was Wednesday; he had to work early the next morning. He went out, got into his car, and started for Morro Vermelho.

On a Saturday night when they were staying in the slum, Ademar stood outside the house talking with Nádia. It was before Gilsa had started going back there alone, and Ademar had begun to notice that Nelson Braga came by the house when they were there. Gilsa paid no attention, but Ademar did not like Nelson. Standing on the porch of the house, he said so to Nádia.

"He's a bastard," Nádia said.

Ademar looked at her. He knew about Nelson; it was Nádia he saw. He said, "Are you going to take the law entry exams?"

"If I can pay for the course."

He spoke quietly. "Will you let me pay?"

She looked at him, watching, something fierce in her eyes. For a minute she didn't speak.

"Yes," she said.

He saw Nelson's laughing face coming toward them.

Ademar was tired after the drive from Rio Bonito but, climbing the hill alone at night, he felt alive. He passed a booth where men stood drinking *cachaça*, and they greeted him by name. He felt suddenly happy. Even when he saw Nelson Braga on the porch of the house with Gilsa, the happiness remained.

"Ademar!"

He heard Nádia's voice and saw her moving toward him out of shadow. Gilsa, separate, wary, leaning against the thin porch railing, looked out at him. Nelson Braga turned, smiling.

Nádia took hold of Ademar's arm.

"Nothing's happened," she said softly.

"Nothing?"

"Not what you're thinking." She waited and watched him. Then she suddenly laughed, a soft, bitter laugh. "If it had, Nelson wouldn't still be around."

Ademar shrugged and moved toward the house.

Later, in the back room, Ademar spoke gently to Gilsa. He asked her to go home with him. In the morning he left and drove back to Rio Bonito alone.

3

He had persuaded the other members of his firm, who were his cousins, to build the small manufacturing facility near Morro Vermelho. Now a young assistant stood beside him, a map laid out on the table.

"The municipal government is enthusiastic, Dr. Ademar. They suggest three alternative sites."

"And the one I suggested?"

"At the bottom of the hill? They'd have to tear down the samba school. They're willing to do it."

He held Nelson Braga's kingdom in his hand. Everything that made Ademar Ademar, that made Nelson Braga only Nelson Braga—wealth, position, power—called him to crush the kingdom. He stood leaning over the table, looking down at the map.

"Are you all right, Dr. Ademar?"

He looked up and saw the young man's face, worried, attentive. Ademar smiled.

"Yes," he said. "Pick one of the alternative sites."

A few minutes later he left his office.

It was still afternoon when he reached the bottom of the hill. He parked the car and started climbing, noticing again the garbage, the filthy streams of sewage. He thought, *this* is the kingdom, but his mind confused Gilsa into everything. Without Gilsa he would have no place here, here where he felt alive.

He saw eyes watching him up the hill. A few greetings were uttered, then suddenly cut short. His presence tensed along the hill like electricity. He wasn't even surprised to see Nelson Braga come hurrying out of his father-in-law's house.

"Ademar," Nelson said, smiling. He stopped on the porch and Ademar stepped in front of him. Nelson was taller, but Ademar was fighting for what he needed.

With a swift movement Ademar grabbed Nelson's shirt and hurled him against the porch railing. The railing broke and Nelson went through, falling into mud and garbage. He lay there a minute and then stood up, covered with filth, looking like an absurd Carnaval figure.

"Son of a bitch, Ademar..."

He stopped. Ademar was looking down from the porch, his eyes cold.

"If you come near her again," Ademar said, "I'll kill you."

Gilsa was standing behind him. As Ademar turned, her eyes met his, waiting. He walked over to her, his eyes caught up in her eyes. She reached out and touched the upper part of his arm, gently. A slight smile traced her lips, lit up her eyes.

He felt his own smile answering hers. He was aware of his heart, running and jumping, stumbling like a boy playing outdoors. *This* is the kingdom, he thought, but again he was confused, dazzled by sunlight. He wanted to talk, to let his heart flow out to her, but his tongue and mouth and throat were all awkward, out of place.

Her smile grew slightly, her eyes warmed.

"Do you want to go home?" he asked. The words came from deep in his chest, half catching in his throat.

She nodded.

He turned and started walking, and she walked with him, hand in hand, down toward the car.

COME INTO MY HOUSE AND STAY
(Rio de Janeiro, 1976)

His name was Rosenthal.

During the nineteen-thirties, his father, an American engineer, had been sent to China. There his father met and married a Chinese woman. Later the couple returned to the United States. Rosenthal was their only child.

In physical appearance, Rosenthal took after his mother. He looked definitely Asian. People he met thought it was uproariously funny for a Chinese man to be named Rosenthal. Rosenthal did not think it was funny.

He came to Brazil because of Lydia. He had known Lydia in college and had been in love with her. Lydia's Irish skin and gray eyes, her golden hair that caught light like a halo, sparked a dream in Rosenthal's methodical soul. Rosenthal was not given to dreams.

Lydia was his friend, but was not in love with him — women generally weren't. She gave her love to Touhy Saint, handsome, blue-eyed, considered likely to succeed. She and Touhy were married right after college. Touhy began promoting businesses that made him a great deal of money; Lydia did volunteer work for the Catholic Church.

Four years later their daughter was born and Touhy left Lydia. She was slapped in the face by pain, and she stood back from it in awe. She named her daughter Rachel because it made her think of weeping.

She was a deeply religious, active Catholic. She decided she wanted to be a missionary, and she started contacting everyone she knew who could help her. The Church was hesitant; its old bones shuddered at the thought of a separated woman representing it. But the ripples of the Second Vatican Council were reaching out to the parishes, bringing with them a feeling that perhaps one did not have to be a priest or nun to be religious. Besides, there was something indomitable about Lydia, a feeling of expectation, an assumption that the right thing would be done, a call of God in her eyes. At last a priest she knew found a place for her in Brazil.

Within a year after arriving in Rio de Janeiro, she was living in the slums. To her it was the only thing to do. She had a small salary from the church agency for which she worked and her parents sent her an allowance from home. It was more than enough. She rented a four room shanty and was the richest person in her neighborhood.

She started taking in children. Emaciated mothers she had never seen would arrive at her door with scrawny, starving infants, bloated bellied toddlers, and beg her to take them. She took them, cleaned them, fed them, loved them. Soon, counting Rachel, there were ten.

About this time a young Brazilian community organizer told her it was paternalistic to take in the children. He was very young and very sincere. She laughed and said she would rather be paternalistic than let a child starve. She won the argument because the community organizer was in love with her. But she began to look for other ways to take care of children.

The priests she worked with were worried about her; they told her, quite accurately, that it wasn't safe to live where she lived. The middle-class Brazilians she met politely shunned her; it confused them that she identified with the poor when she didn't have to, made them feel guilty, brought out their nagging fear of being poor. Americans in Rio, who were not threatened by poverty and who, in their comfortable apartments, often discussed the injustice of the social system, accepted her as a curiosity. They thought she was strange.

So did the people in her neighborhood. But in their hard way they loved her and took care of her. She was never molested or robbed. She was the only person in the slum who would go out of her house and leave the door unlocked.

Even the police left her alone. Had she been a man she might have been arrested, killed. She was a woman. They could accuse her of nothing more subversive than living the word of God which, God knows, was subversive enough but left no real grounds for accusation. Besides, she had a way of marching into the offices of government officials, sometimes with a small flock of neighbors in her wake, and openly requesting, even demanding, that something be done. Her assumption that they would do the right thing took the officials by surprise, and often they ended up doing it. Reluctantly they respected her, even liked her.

Her daughter, Rachel, grew like a weed. Lydia's mother wrote worried letters asking how Lydia could let Rachel grow up in the slums. "Surely, Mother," Lydia wrote back, "it doesn't hurt to raise her as a Christian."

But she didn't neglect Rachel, or any of her children. She kept them clean and well fed, clothed them, tutored them, played with them, sent them to the public school. And her circle of protection extended to the whole neighborhood.

She argued with mothers about nutrition, taught them hygiene, persuaded them to send their children to school, helped them get government documents. She would walk into a shack where a drunken man was beating his wife, where everyone was afraid to enter, would stop the beating and argue the man sober. She was fearless. A hundred times she should have been knifed or shot. She never was.

Lydia had been in Brazil ten years when Touhy Saint died. He had just left a cocktail party and drove his Porsche into a cement wall. He was drunk. *Business Week* lamented the passing of a rising young entrepreneur. Lydia, whom he had never divorced, inherited a hundred thousand dollars. She accepted it as she accepted everything, openly and without undue concern, arranging with a broker in Philadelphia to send her small monthly stipends.

Rosenthal, who in his careful way read *Business Week* cover to cover, saw the item about Touhy's death. He thought of Lydia and the old dream began to stir in his soul. Like his father, he had become an engineer, although he was more into the business end of engineering than his father had been. Rather than going to distant lands, he became production manager for a Southern California appliances manufacturer. The appliances his company made were very practical. Rosenthal was fairly well off and had never married.

He decided to write Lydia. Methodically, he set about finding her address. In the process he learned about her separation from Touhy and her move to Brazil.

His first letter was very careful, very safe. He had recently heard of Touhy's death, he said, and expressed sympathy. He hoped that she was doing well. He might be traveling to Brazil in a few months and would very much like to see her. He hoped she would write him to let him know if that were possible. In the meantime, he wished her the best and signed, after some hesitation, "Your Friend, Fred."

Rosenthal signed as Fred because that's what Lydia had always called him. Frederick was, in fact, his first name, and he signed checks and business letters Frederick C. Rosenthal. The C was for Chung. But neither Rosenthal nor anyone else ever thought of him as anything other than Rosenthal. Only Lydia had used his Christian name.

Lydia's response, when it came a month or so later, was warm, cheerful, and friendly. Like everything she did, her letter expanded itself beyond the confines of its pages and came alive. Long, organic, it had clearly been written at several sittings over a period of a couple of weeks and reflected her thoughts and concerns of each moment. It ended, "I'll mail this today, Fred, or you'll never get it. Love, Lydia."

His travel agent had booked him at one of those plush modern hotels on Copacabana beach where the chambermaids earn less in a month than a guest pays for a single night. The desk clerk, who was wondering whether his job was secure enough to move his family out of the slums, saw nothing strange in a Chinese man being named Rosenthal.

Rosenthal's room was large, with a view of the ocean, thick carpets, two queen-sized beds. His flight from Los Angeles had been enormously long. Rosenthal showered and lay down to take a nap.

It was early afternoon when he awoke. He dressed quickly but carefully: permanent-press slacks, sport coat, button-down shirt, bow tie. He took his camera and, putting on a white cap, went downstairs. His clothes were pure Southern California, but people in the lobby assumed that Rosenthal, who was American to his bones, was a Japanese tourist.

He knew that Lydia had no telephone. He had neatly written her address on a small white card. The doorman waved him a taxi. Rosenthal climbed in and showed the address to the driver. The driver looked at it and said something in Portuguese. Rosenthal didn't understand, and the driver called over the doorman and spoke to him, showing him the address. The doorman looked concerned and asked Rosenthal in broken English if he was sure he wanted to go to that address. Rosenthal was sure. The taxi driver shrugged and they started off.

It seemed to Rosenthal that they drove for about an hour, through tunnels and long urban neighborhoods, under hillsides dotted with colorful wooden shacks, then past factories. It would be inaccurate to say that Rosenthal's heart beat faster; it followed its customary measured tick. But his dream glowed.

In her letters, Lydia had mentioned her work and talked a good deal about her neighborhood. She hadn't spoken of it as a slum. For her it wasn't any longer a slum, but a neighborhood, a community of people, good, bad, likable, unlikable. She didn't mention the stench of sewage, the garbage piled thick under the houses, or sharing a bathroom with three families. These things were so much a part of life she didn't think to mention them.

A good American, Rosenthal very seldom thought of poverty. No one he knew was poor. He was aware that Lydia's neighbors were laborers and bus drivers, bricklayers, carpenters, office boys, unemployed. He had wondered vaguely why she lived in a working-class neighborhood.

Suddenly the taxi stopped. They were at the end of a paved street. Rosenthal got out, paid the driver, and the taxi drove off. Rosenthal was standing alone, looking out over a chaotic mass of low wooden shanties. He didn't know where to go.

He became aware of people staring at him, dark faces with large eyes, children's faces and adults', stopped in mid-conversation in front of the low doors, staring out of the gaping wooden windows. They were not hostile stares, only indifferent, as though Rosenthal were from a different planet.

He took the card with Lydia's address out of his pocket. Seeing two gray-haired men who looked, somehow, less foreign, he walked over to them. He spoke to them in English, knowing they wouldn't understand but needing to speak, and pointed to the address. One of the men took the card and studied it laboriously, trying to make out what it said. A small crowd gathered around them. The man motioned to a boy, who came over and said something to the man. Someone said, "Americana?" and Rosenthal nodded and said yes. They indicated he should follow the boy.

The boy started along one of the paths. It had rained that morning and the path was muddy, a filthy stinking mud that vapored in the hot afternoon sun. Everywhere in the mud there was garbage—the bright colored garbage of a capitalist society—labels, cigarette packages, bits of magazines. Here and there they crossed over small streams, littered with trash, the water thick with excrement. Children were filling plastic bottles with water.

The paths seemed to have no organization, splitting, angling, crossing other paths. Rosenthal was hopelessly disoriented, following the boy as an act of faith. The hot sun beat down. Rosenthal was aware of people's eyes staring at him.

His stomach began to churn, the smell, the sun, the confusion closing in on him. Then the boy stopped in front of a house that was a little higher, a little better kept than the rest, although Rosenthal could hardly tell the difference. The boy clapped his hands and called out. The door swung open and Lydia stood there.

It seemed to Rosenthal that the world stood still. He had forgotten how beautiful Lydia was. As happens when one is in love, he had forgotten what she really looked like, her appearance merging into a feeling of warmth and challenge, home and desire. But Rosenthal knew very little about love.

She stepped toward him, smiling. Her hair had a slight streak of gray, her skin glowed, her gray eyes sparkled. She took his hand and led him inside.

The small room had a wooden floor. A refrigerator stood against one wall. Nine or ten people were sitting in the room, their chairs crowded into a circle. They rose as Rosenthal entered; Lydia introduced him to each and each shook his hand. There was a large black man in a black suit, white shirt, and narrow tie, and a young, nervous-looking white man in a beige suit. The others were in work clothes, men of varying ages, a fat middle-aged woman, a younger woman. Rosenthal did not pick up any of their names.

A chair was pushed forward and Rosenthal sat down. The others, also seated, took up a discussion that Rosenthal's arrival seemed to have interrupted. A workman was questioning the nervous young man in the suit. The young man said something. The fat woman began to speak and everyone listened respectfully. A twelve-year-old girl, very white and blonde, pushed into the room carrying a tray of small cups. Rosenthal took one; it was coffee, black, strong, and very sweet. He set it aside. The fat woman stopped speaking.

Then the big man in the black suit began to talk, turning and addressing the nervous man. The big man's voice rolled out like an orator's. He spoke for several minutes. Rosenthal felt sweat trickling down his body. He looked at the faces around him as though he could find some order in them. He glanced toward Lydia, but she was intently into that world which lay beyond his screen of comprehension. He felt alone and confused.

The people were now rising. They stood still, bowed their heads, and the big man said a few quiet words. Then they were shaking one another's hand, patting one another on the shoulder. Someone shook Rosenthal's hand, then another and another. He nodded each time, trying to be correct, polite. Slowly the people left.

He was alone with Lydia. Alone except for the children, who came from the other room. Ten of them, Rosenthal counted, of different ages and colors. Lydia introduced them as her children, and each one greeted him in English.

Rosenthal and Lydia talked. Rosenthal was not one to reminisce; he had nothing to reminisce about. For Lydia the past was unimportant. She was rapt completely in the present, and soon she was telling Rosenthal about it as though he were part of it too. The meeting had been of neighborhood leaders; they had found a lawyer to represent them. Oh—hadn't she told him in her letters?—the land they were on was claimed by a large contractor. It was becoming valuable. The court proceedings were dragging on. The nervous young man was their lawyer. The big black man was the Baptist minister. The rest were neighbors, friends.

Rosenthal listened intently. He did not really understand why she was here, why she felt so strongly about these people. It seemed irrational, but then Rosenthal supposed women were irrational. It was interesting, but it made him uncomfortable.

"Come on." Lydia suddenly stood up. "Let me show you around."

Rosenthal thought she meant around her house, but she didn't. They walked out the front door. She led him down the pathways, and once again a feeling of chaos suffocated him. But Lydia was unaware, chatting pleasantly. She stopped and introduced him to people, as though forgetting he didn't speak Portuguese, talking to the people at length. She took him by the Baptist church, which was neatly painted, its tiny dirt yard swept clean. She showed him an upraised area where there were water faucets and concrete basins. "We did that," she said proudly. She pointed out houses that neighbors had helped each other build. It all looked wretched and filthy to Rosenthal.

Night was falling as she showed Rosenthal how to get back to his hotel. She never rode in taxis, she said, but she showed him where to get a bus and waited with him until it came. He asked her if he could come by next evening and take her out—"out of here," he almost said, but he said, "out to dinner." That would be lovely, she said. He got on the bus.

He got out of the bus as soon as he could and took a cab. When he reached his hotel room he removed his clothes and neatly folded them, isolating them in a corner of the bathroom floor. He took a long, warm shower.

The taxi driver screeched on the brakes. It was almost evening again, the shadows long. Lydia had agreed to meet him at the entry to the slum and they would go out to dinner. Rosenthal, again dressed in a sport coat, bow tie, and slacks, was planning methodically how he would order.

They were not at the place where he was supposed to meet Lydia. The driver said something excitedly and got out of the cab. Rosenthal got out too. Ahead, great black billows of smoke were rising into the sky. Rosenthal felt suddenly afraid.

Several other cars had stopped and the other drivers were talking with Rosenthal's driver. Rosenthal went over and told his driver to take him further. The driver understood but shook his head. Rosenthal turned and started walking down the road.

In fifteen minutes he was at the edge of the slum. He could see the smoke was rising from it. Here and there he could see flames. The houses near him had not been touched by fire, but people were hauling things out of them—televisions, furniture, mattresses—and carrying them to the far side of the road. Without thinking, he started down the path that he and the boy had taken the day before. It was filled with people coming the other way, carrying their belongings. He pushed forward. He spoke to himself, bringing the rational part of his mind back to its natural dominance, and tried to remember the paths he had followed yesterday. He turned down one and was soon hopelessly lost.

The smoke was thicker now. There was almost no one on the pathways. Ahead, he saw a man emptying a bottle of water on a wooden house. It struck him as a pathetic gesture and he moved forward to help. Suddenly the man stooped, lit a match, and set it to the house. The house burst into flames and Rosenthal stopped, appalled, realizing that the liquid in the bottle had not been water. The man stood and faced him; he was wearing a mask and had a pistol looped through his belt. Rosenthal turned and ran.

He didn't know how he did it, but a few moments later he was standing in front of Lydia's house. The pathway in front of it was deserted, but the houses were not on fire. The door to her house was open and Rosenthal stepped inside.

Lydia was in the living room, putting some papers into a small satchel. She looked up. Her face was pale, her gray eyes blazing.

"Fred," she said.

"The children?" he asked.

"They've gone. I'm going too. Here, take this." She thrust the satchel and a bag of books into his hands, then stooped and grabbed up a plastic bag bulging with small items. "Let's go."

They walked out the door. The pathway was still calm, deserted except for a single figure in the direction away from the road, carefully pouring liquid along the row of houses. It was not the same man Rosenthal had seen, but Rosenthal knew what the man was doing. He tried to turn Lydia away, but she had seen too.

She was angry. She started toward the figure and Rosenthal followed her. The man lit a match and Lydia yelled something at him. He looked up, surprised, and his match went out. He stood up and pulled out a revolver, waving for them to go away. Rosenthal stopped, but Lydia moved forward. She was talking now, a stream of Portuguese words flowing quietly and firmly from her, her eyes on the man's. She had moved quite close to him.

Suddenly the man lifted his revolver and whipped the barrel across her face. Lydia reeled back and Rosenthal, dropping the bag of books, stepped forward and caught her in his arms. Her face was bleeding and her eyes were on the man, wide with pain. The man fired a shot at the dirt and then pointed his gun at Rosenthal. Rosenthal put his arm around Lydia's shoulder and they turned and walked away. Behind them they could feel the houses going up in flames.

Only a few stragglers were coming out of the slum. Everyone else, men, women, children, stood across the road where Rosenthal and Lydia also stood, watching with dead faces as the flames lit against the night.

"No one would do that," Rosenthal said. He was watching the flames and his words were lost in the night. His brain, deadened by fear and excitement, began to move slowly. Wrong. Yes, it was all wrong. And yet... He thought of fire, cleansing the slum, burning out the filth, the rottenness. One could build streets, neat little streets of orderly houses, cement, chase out the filth, the wretchedness. His mind was moving steadily now, a smooth machine.

Then he saw the Baptist minister, looming like a giant on the road. The minister turned toward the people and his voice boomed out a singe phrase larger than life. There was silence for a moment, then someone near Rosenthal repeated the phrase, then another and another. He heard Lydia speak the words softly.

"What are they saying?" Rosenthal asked.

"'Forgive them, God. They don't know what they're doing.'"

Her voice was quiet. The flames licked up toward the sky. Rosenthal stood and watched, bewildered into heights of incomprehension.

THE HEALER
(The Slums Outside Rio de Janeiro, 1999)

I was surprised when I received a message that Pastor Eugênio wanted to speak to me. We had never been close—indeed, he had always made it clear he wanted as little contact as possible with Catholic clergy. I remembered him as a small but strongly built man in his mid-fifties, his bronze head balding, his face humorless but sincere, dressed in the dark suit and white shirt that the older Evangelical preachers usually wore, clutching a black Bible and presiding over his small church at the edge of the slums. Not an educated man, but he knew his Bible. He had a reputation for being a healer.

His attitude toward Catholics wasn't unusual. In the huge, sprawling, poverty-ridden suburbs of Rio de Janeiro, we try to be ecumenical—God knows, with parishes of forty thousand people, we need to cooperate all we can. We don't have enough workers, even with the many lay staff and volunteers. The Evangelical churches have been proliferating steadily.

The smaller, more radical of these churches fill a need. They forbid smoking, drinking, dancing, gambling—and thus protect the men in the slums from the temptations that surround them. While the theology may be questionable—stressing the fear of hell—the impact is notable. What slum woman, finding her drunken, philandering, irresponsible husband turned to a sober, faithful, hardworking man, is going to question the theology behind the change?

But to these little churches, the Catholic Church is a giant, accounting at least nominally for eighty percent of the people, having a structure of diocese, seminaries, religious orders. And it is from a nominal Catholicism that most of the faithful of these small churches have been recruited, so there is a need to keep distance. These small churches must see ecumenical outreach by the Church the way a rabbit would view a proposal for cooperation from a lion, and a lion with a bloody jaw at that!

I had worked in that parish fifteen years. Now, after five years of vocation work stateside, I was visiting again for a couple of weeks before taking up my new duties in northern Brazil. I had been in town several days, talking with parishioners, visiting the youth center, walking the streets and greeting old faces, when a woman came by the parish house and left the message that Pastor Eugênio wanted to see me when it was convenient.

There was no urgency to the message, so it was a couple of mornings later that I walked over to the small church. Pastor Eugênio, I knew, lived near his church, and although I had never been to his house, I had no trouble finding it. It was a simple, one-story row house built in the 1930s, better than most in the surrounding slums, but certainly unpretentious. I rang the bell and, after a few moments, heard footsteps on the tiled floor inside. The door was opened by a woman in her thirties who, smiling, said she was the pastor's daughter. She led me into the front room and said she would let the pastor know I was here.

The room was like thousands of others in Brazil. A brown vinyl sofa on black metal legs, two matching vinyl chairs, a picture of a blond Jesus and framed quotations from the Bible (in a Catholic home it would have been a dark-haired Mary and framed saints), the ceramic tiled floor with a geometrical pattern of black on beige. A bookstand with knickknacks, family pictures, an artificial flower in a vase, a Bible, concordance, dictionary, and half a dozen other books.

I heard a slight sound behind me and turned to see an old man come into the room. What little hair he had was white, and he was stooped and frail. It took me a moment until I was startled to recognize that this was Pastor Eugênio—the strong, determined, dynamic man I remembered.

"Thank you for coming," he said, shaking my hand. His hand, though it had lost flesh, was still firm and strong. I told him I was glad to come.

He nodded, and invited me to sit in one of the chairs. He sat down on the sofa—in the small room we were only a few feet apart—and, while his daughter served us coffee and then left us, he asked about my trip, then about the United States. They were ordinary questions— polite conversation—and he was only half listening to the answers. He appeared distracted and I had the impression that, having invited me there, he wasn't quite sure what he wanted to say, or how to start. Finally he said abruptly, "I asked you to come here because I always felt you were a good man."

The compliment surprised me. After five years away, my Portuguese was still a little rusty, and my tongue felt awkward, but I fielded it as best I could.

"Who of us is good? We most of us do the best we can."

He nodded again. My eyes were becoming accustomed to the changes in his face, and I could begin to see more clearly the Pastor Eugênio I had known. He still seemed humorless—that had not changed.

"There is something I need to say." He paused for a moment, looking not at me but slightly to my left, toward the light of the front window. "One does not... cannot burden one's people with these things," he looked at me briefly and I nodded understanding. "And these other pastors…" He waved his hand as if brushing something away. "There is no one…no one…."

"You know I am a healer."

"Yes," I said.

"This is a gift from God. It came to me early—when I was a boy. I would pray over people and they would be healed. Little things at first, but the power grew as I grew in faith and prayer and scripture. And I was true to it—I never took money for healing. I started working with an old pastor in the countryside—when I had learned my scripture, I felt God was calling me here to the city. There is so much pain here…."

He was silent for a moment, still looking toward the light of the window.

"I came here and started this little church. It was a raw, new slum then, with people coming from the countryside like I had come, families broken by drink and displacement. The church drew people, and I took my living out of what the church brought in—a worker is worth his wages. But I never took money for healing— any gifts that came that way went to help the poor. Anything else would have been an abomination."

He glanced at me and I nodded. He looked away again.

"But there is another thing besides money. I say I am a healer—but that's wrong. Jesus is the healer, and I am only a tool in his hands. But there is pride in that—and there is danger. The devil tries to make us healers think that it is *we* who are important, bloating us up with self-importance. All my life I have struggled against that, fought and prayed and fasted to remember that I am only a sinful man. I wrestled that until...."

"There was in our congregation a widow who had only a son. You know that in these past ten years the drug trafficking has grown, has taken over everywhere. Many of the young men have been drawn into it, and this son—Ismael—was one of them. He drifted away from church when he was about fourteen. He lived at home with his mother, as most of them do, but she had no control over him. He had money to spend and carried a pistol. They live fast and die young, these young men, and God have mercy on their souls.

"Two years ago the mother came to me in tears. Ismael had been in a gunfight—one of these between the gangs. He was shot in the spine. I rushed with the mother to the hospital. We prayed over the boy—he was twenty-one then, and no longer really a boy. He lived, but was paralyzed from the neck down."

Pastor Eugênio's tongue dampened his parched lips. He sat a moment, as though remembering.

"The mother took him home, and I visited frequently. At first the boy seemed dazed at being alive, but then as days passed he became angry and bitter. Better to be dead, he said, than prisoner in a useless body. He railed at his mother as to why she hadn't let him die. His mouth spat venomous, spiteful words.

"One day, when I was visiting, praying over him, he was especially foul and abusive. His words flowed out evil. Suddenly his mother broke in, her voice almost tearful, 'Son, don't talk like that. Don't you know Pastor Eugênio can heal you?'

"He looked up at me then, half-defiantly—but that defiance that often hides hope.

"'Can you heal me?' he asked.

"There is a certain sense that comes with the gift—grows with it. Sometimes you know that a sickness, a condition, will not be healed. I had never dealt with paralysis, but I—Christ through me—had healed things as bad or worse. At that moment I sensed this could be healed.

"'Ismael,' I said. 'It is not I but Christ who heals. I am His tool. If you want to be healed, you must first repent and recognize God's hand in all that has happened to you.'

"He looked at me hard. 'I will think about that,' he said.

"When I came back the next morning, he looked serious. 'Pastor,' he said, 'I have thought about it. I know I did evil and that God punished me. He paralyzed me so that I can do no more wrong. I repent and ask to be healed.'

"I thought his mother was going to burst with joy. I felt a victory for the Lord in my heart. We set the prayer session for that evening—I called in six or eight people who have helped me in the past. We stood around his bed and offered up thanks and praise. We quoted scripture and laid on our hands. I felt the power surge through me—the others felt the same. We finished and drew away our hands.

"And nothing. Nothing happened at all."

"Of course, this wasn't the first time a cure hadn't been accomplished in the first session. I had never felt anything quite like it before, but we decided that the Lord was asking us to work a little harder. We scheduled another session, then another. Three—four times a week we prayed over him, and still there was no progress. Through it all he remained patient and calm—as though he knew, somehow, the cure would happen.

"One morning when I came to visit him I bumped into another young man coming out the door. I knew him—his name was João Jorge—one of Ismael's former friends, a small drug peddler.

"'What are you doing here?' I asked.

"He held up his two hands. 'Don't be angry with me, Pastor. Just visiting the sick. It's one of the corporal works of mercy, they tell us.'

"He was mocking me, I knew. It stung all the more because of my sense that I was failing—that the cure I had been praying for wasn't taking place.

"I redoubled my efforts. I spent two days a week fasting, and often prayed all night. My work at the church suffered—but I felt it was suffering for a just cause. Time and time again, as we prayed over him, I felt the power surge through me, *knew* that the cure could be achieved. Yet nothing happened.

"And still the boy—Ismael—was patient, waiting.

"One night, deep in prayer, it came to me that God did not want this cure. I argued with God, as Abraham argued. I spent the night wrestling with God, as Abraham wrestled. At dawn, in desperation, I called out, 'Lord, all the community is looking on us, watching us. They are beginning to laugh. Would you make a mockery of my faith?'

"That evening, exhausted, I dragged myself to the session to pray over Ismael. Once again I felt the power surge through me. When we finished, we stood back from the bed. Ismael moved his right hand."

"I can't describe the joy that swept through us that evening. The healing had started—and from there it went smoothly. In a week, Ismael was moving both arms, in another week, his feet. Gradually he regained strength and the use of his limbs.

"The church, too, thrived. My passing neglect of it was now recompensed tenfold. As word of the miracle spread, the services were filled with people praising God. We added new services—new healings took place, and miracles of conversion.

"And then…and then….

"Two weeks after Ismael had completely regained the use of his body—agile and limber as new—late at night, he took an automatic pistol and two of the most vicious thugs in the neighborhood and went into the neighborhood of the man who had shot him. They broke into his house and killed everyone who was there—women, children, old people—except the man himself, who they shot in the spine and paralyzed."

"He had been planning it all along, you see. Using João Jorge as his messenger. Waiting, waiting with the patience of the devil, knowing he would be cured."

Pastor Eugênio stopped speaking. The room was wrapt in silence.

"And Ismael?" I asked.

"Dead," he answered. "His crime was a brutal one, even for the drug traffickers. The local gang leader wouldn't protect him. The other gang came to his house and executed him. They made a point of sparing his mother—if you can call it that—saying they would not sink to his level."

He was silent again for nearly a minute. I remained silent with him.

"I did an evil thing," he said at last.

"But surely you did what you thought was best—praying for a healing."

He shook his head.

"No," he said. "I knew God didn't want this healing. It was my own pride. I had said I would do it, and I was afraid of being laughed at, being mocked. I threw that in God's face."

Again there was silence.

"But now you have recognized you were wrong," I said. "You've repented."

"I do not feel it is enough."

I wanted to lift my hand in absolution, but that wouldn't have been appropriate. I whispered a brief absolution in my mind.

The silence in the room had become peaceful. Now that he had finished talking, his eyes were turned fully toward me. I thought I saw a seeking, an expectation there.

"Will you pray with me about it?" I asked.

He nodded. I moved forward in my chair and reached out my two hands. He grasped them with his own, and we bowed our heads.

COLORS
(Belém, 1984)

Orange, yellow, blue, green, red—
"Colors, Chico," my grandfather said. "God loves colors." His big cinnamon-colored hand guided the wide paint brush over the weathered wooden wall. He laughed his deep laugh.

I was ten years old. I looked up at the yellow paint, brightening the gray wooden wall of our shack, and I laughed with him.

Colors. He always talked about colors. The colors of the Amazon rainforest and savannah lands where he had grown up. Blue and yellow of the big macaws that always flew in pairs—male and female. Red and green parrots, black toucans with orange beaks, a flock of green parakeets alighting in a single tree and turning it into a living, chirping miracle. Copper-colored guará wolves—tall and thin and graceful. And the flowers—red-orange-yellow dangling heliconia, bright red beaks of bird-of-paradise flowers, white and pink lotus floating on the ponds.

There was little enough color in the slum where we lived, in the big city of Belém near the mouth of the

Amazon River. Gray wooden unpainted shacks on gray-black mud streets. A few bedraggled plants in the tiny yards, a few caged songbirds. In those days—the early 1980s—clothing was expensive, so it was worn until the colors were washed away.

My grandfather, Francisco Ramos, was born on the Amazonian frontier, in the rain forests and grasslands east of the Araguaia River. He grew up on the land—farming and cattle raising—married and had his own small farm, with a dozen head of cattle. He especially loved working with cattle, and always kept the strong, wiry, self-reliant bearing of a cowhand. Maybe that's what saw him through when so many others stumbled and were lost. That, and his love of people, and the deep joy that was down inside him. And colors.

He spoke often of his boyhood, of working the cattle, even of the crops—but he almost never spoke of the troubled times and why the family left the land. "Bad time—everybody has bad times," he would say. "Remember the good times—let the bad times go."

It was only later, when I was studying at the university, that I began to understand. In the late 1960s, the land along the frontier started to become valuable. Agents—known as *grileiros*—began buying land for big companies and wealthy individuals. Small farmers usually had no legal title—they had been on the land for years, and had legal rights of ownership, but they rarely understood the law. Nor was there much law to help them—the few lawyers worked with the *grileiros*, and the judges were indifferent or intimidated.

The *grileiros'* methods were not gentle. They would start by offering a small amount of cash for land—and many families took it. A little money seems a lot to a dirt farmer who has never lived in a city, paid rent, bought food. The farmers who would not sell out began to have trouble—crops burned, houses burned. Men beaten up. Those who continued to resist—or led the resistance—were sometimes killed.

As I said, my grandfather never spoke of it. But he had a scar in the upper corner of his chest, near his shoulder, and another in his back—where a bullet had gone through. My Uncle Manuel told me that he held out until the end—almost the last small landholder in his district—and that it was only as he lay wounded, my grandmother in tears imploring him to give up, that he signed away his land.

And so—like many others—he moved his family into Belém—into the fast-growing slums along the river's edge, where arriving families built houses on poles over the sluggish backwaters, then bribed garbage truck drivers to dump trash as filler, covering it over with a thin layer of soil. That landfill was the ground of our neighborhood of unpainted wooden shacks.

Many of the men who made this move crumbled. Strong taciturn country men, used to providing for their families, they came to the city and looked for work. Illiterate, with no urban skills, they were fortunate if they could get jobs as unskilled construction helpers— the lowest of the low—earning less than a dollar a day. Earning little, often out of work, they began to lose faith in themselves. Their wives—skilled in cooking, washing, childcare—often found better jobs. No longer the provider, no longer respecting themselves, the men would take to drinking, gambling, hanging around. Because they did not respect themselves, their children did not respect them, and went their own way in this strange urban world that their fathers didn't understand. The fathers, broken and belittled, drifted into irrelevance, some abandoning their families completely.

But my grandfather was one of the few who held on. He was in his early forties, fully mature, and had learned his self worth working with cattle in the grasslands. He was stubborn in his way—he wouldn't give up—but also knew how to adapt. He learned to read—not fluently, but sufficiently to decipher simple instructions. Gradually he rose from unskilled laborer to foreman, picking up skills along the way—learning to paint, to lay bricks, even to do a little wiring and plumbing.

The family he brought with him from the country consisted of his elderly aunt—a lively old woman who lived with us (she died when I was sixteen), his wife—my grandmother, his son and three daughters—the eldest married to my Uncle Manuel. Not all of the family made it. After a few months, their son left to try his luck in the new capital—Brasília—and was never heard from again. My mother, the youngest daughter, dazzled by the freedom of the city, took to staying out late, drinking, hanging around with men. Two years after they arrived, when she was nineteen, I was born. A year later she was dead—killed unintentionally by a wild gunshot in a barroom brawl.

Nobody knew anything about my father. "He must have been a good man," my grandfather said to me once, putting his hand on my shoulder, "to have such a good son."

That day of the painting, my grandfather came jauntily home, carrying a burlap bag. He was not yet fifty-five, though he looked ten years older—his graying hair above his lean high-cheek-boned face. Like most of our people, he was a mixture of Indian and Portuguese, with probably a little African stirred in. He had sparkling dark brown eyes.

He set the bag down and it clanked as it hit the ground. My grandmother was coming out of the shack to meet him. She was a sturdy woman, a head shorter than he was, with a quiet sense of humor. She was deeply religious, and each October led us all, walking barefoot, among white and yellow flowers and multi-colored banners, in the procession that carried the white-and-gold robed statue of Our Lady of Nazareth through the streets of Belém. My grandmother was barefoot now, and wearing a rose-colored dress my grandfather had bought her.

"What is this?" she asked, looking at the bag.

My grandfather opened the bag. Inside were five one-gallon cans and two paint brushes.

"We finished painting," he said. He had been working the last few weeks, remodeling a pre-school in one of the wealthy neighborhoods. "They gave me what was left over."

She reached over and picked up one of the cans. It seemed light.

"There isn't much left."

"About an eighth of a can in that one, a little more in some of the others."

"What are you going to do with it?"

"Paint the front of the house. There should be just about enough for that."

She looked again at the cans. "But they're five different colors," she said.

"That's right," my grandfather answered.

My grandmother smiled and shook her head.

So we painted, my grandfather and I. To the left of the door, he painted bright yellow, while I painted the door blue. The three window frames and the wall over the door we painted red—we didn't have much red. To the right of the door we painted neat vertical stripes of orange and green.

And then we stood back and looked at it—my grandfather, my grandmother, his old aunt—and a whole bunch of neighbors who had gathered to watch and talk and comment. It was beautiful, my grandfather said, and to me it was beautiful—then, and in my memory ever since.

Orange, yellow, blue, green, red. Colors. God loves colors, my grandfather always said.

SWITZERLAND
(Recife, 1993)

The shiny red adhesive Swiss flag, with its cross in white, was a patch of bright, clean color on the dusty black dashboard of the old brown Chevette. Seen through the half-open smudged window of the car, parked in the grime and noise of the Recife market, the flag was a window whispering into the hot Brazilian afternoon a cool, crisp breeze from the Alps.

Maria Amélia stood by her car, her arms gesturing rapidly as she negotiated with Seu Zé Paulo the sale of a trunk-load of cheap plastic toys smuggled from Paraguay. She was a dynamic, compact woman in her late thirties, a little overweight but well-made and good-looking, her dark brown hair slightly awry, her eyes bright. She was a savvy trader. The deal with Seu Zé Paulo—part of her network of allies, rivals, cohorts, competitors—was soon closed. Bills passed from his hands to hers, she opened the trunk, he unloaded three cartons onto the sidewalk and called over a boy to carry them, she closed the trunk, chatting with him now about their families, both smiling (the deal had—as usual—been mutually satisfactory). Car keys in hand, she moved toward the door of the car, laughing with him over a small joke. In all this she did not glance at—even think of—the Swiss flag; but it was always there, her talisman, her window into another life.

Maria Amélia was of a long tradition of Brazilian commercial women. She and her husband, Jorge, were known in the market—having their own stand and trading wholesale with other stand owners. Even Jorge, himself no mean trader, stood in awe of Maria Amélia. Like most women of her kind, she was commercially fierce. She had a ring of protection—Jorge, their two children, her widowed mother, her crippled uncle, the Sisters of Jesus Crucified and their orphanage, old Father Julio. Those within the circle were selflessly served and kept from harm. Beyond that lay her network of allies and competitors, treated with mutual wariness and respect. And, beyond them, the world at large—where Maria Amélia's ferocity awed even Jorge—a land that, within rough ethical borders and a slight nod to the law, was there to be plundered, despoiled, even cheated—though never cheated where it violated her word, only to the extent that it agreed to be cheated. It was enemy territory where, she felt, one either won or lost. Yet, even there, she could at times bestow acts of unexpected generosity or kindness, acts that surprised her associates, her husband, even herself.

All this was carried out in the busy working- and lower-middle-class markets of greater Recife. Buying at bargain prices, bartering, selling wholesale to other stand owners, selling retail at their own stand, arranging side deals wherever they were profitable. Payments to the police to look after their stand, payments to the tax inspectors to look the other way, payments to the neighborhood *justiceiros* to keep street-kids and petty thieves away. Up at four in the morning and out on the streets with Jorge to pick up goods—plastics from Paraguay, clothes smuggled up from southern Brazil without paying the merchandise taxes, shoes from a local unregistered maker, blue jeans from another local maker—but bearing the label of an internationally-known fashion house, pirated videos and CDs, scarves, swimsuits, underwear. No stolen goods— they didn't mess with people from those circles—nothing immoral—Maria Amélia and Jorge were both, in their way, strict moralists—nothing more illegal than contraband and tax evasion, the general rule in their world. Trades made early, then to the stand at seven a.m. to check on the woman—a cousin of Jorge's—who worked the stand for fair pay that was nowhere registered in legal documents. Maria Amélia had eagle eyes and a calculator mind—any missing cent had to be accounted for—on that basis, she and Jorge's cousin got along very well. Half an hour later, she and Jorge were off again—now together, now separately, depending on the day and the deals— delivering, negotiating, trading—stopping for a short lunch, often grabbed at a market stall talking to an ally, then onto an afternoon of deals—back to the stand at least once more to count the take, roughly inventory the stock, deliver goods for the next day's sale—before heading home at six p.m. and flopping down—both of them—on the red vinyl sofa in the tiny living room.

In the morning, after they were gone, Maria Amélia's mother got the children out of bed, washed, breakfasted, sent to school. It was a private neighborhood school— costing about forty dollars a month for each child—not the best of schools, Maria Amélia knew, but better than the public schools and the best they could do. School lasted four hours and the children came home for lunch, then studied and played in the afternoon under their grandmother's watchful eye. Maria Amélia thanked God for her mother—a healthy, happy woman in her late fifties—for her care of the children, the clothes washed in the small washing-machine they'd bartered for, the supper ready when Maria Amélia and Jorge got home.

This was their life. Maria Amélia complained of the pace, the rushing about, the endless work. But she loved it—loved the motion, the quick thinking, the deals. And, when it all got to be too much, there was the red adhesive Swiss flag shining on their dashboard, and a single tourist poster of the Swiss Alps wafting a breeze of cool, mountain air into their tiny living room.

This was their life, and it would have remained much the same if it weren't for the raffle. Each year the Sisters of Jesus Crucified held a raffle to support their orphanage, and each year Maria Amélia and Jorge bought two books of tickets for themselves, as well as another dozen or so they sold to people in their network. One year they won a set of hand towels, and another a couple of bottles of wine—never enough to equal the value of the tickets they purchased. But that wasn't the point—the Sisters and their orphanage were within the circle of protection, and were to be supported, donated to, helped.

Saturday afternoon, Maria Amélia and Jorge swung by and spent a couple of hours at the Sisters' annual bazaar—pastries for sale baked by the Sisters and their friends, handicrafts made by the older orphans, little food stands, rummage donated for resale, young people selling the final raffle tickets. Wealthy and middle-class and working-class people wandering through the stands, buying things they really didn't want or need to help the Sisters. Maria Amélia picked up a few things that would be marginally useful—an embroidered tablecloth, a colored candle, some decorated soap. Greeting and kissing the sisters on each cheek, smiling at the people helping in the stands, then off away to do a dozen things that needed doing—there were always at least a dozen—before heading home for a few hours with the children.

So she was not there for the raffle. It was only Sunday evening that the telephone rang at home and Maria Amélia went to answer it—Sister Joana telling her that she had won one of the best prizes, donated by the Suttlier Travel Agency: round trip tickets for two, and four nights in a hotel in Zurich.

The tickets could be used any time in the next twelve months. Maria Amélia did not immediately plan a date, which would have surprised Jorge except that he had learned long ago not to be surprised. Being married to Maria Amélia, Jorge had learned, was much like surfing the waves off Recife—something he had done much of as a teenager. It required skill and balance, but most of all riding the wave—and it was never dull.

Instead, Maria Amélia plunged into getting all the information she could. This was like her, Jorge thought. On Monday she went into Suttlier and returned with details of the prize she had won, airline schedules, hotel descriptions, and pamphlets on Switzerland. On Tuesday she found out about passports and visas— neither of them had ever traveled outside Brazil. On Wednesday she bought a travel guide. By Saturday she had figured out how they could extend their stay from four to eight days at minimal extra cost. She was calculating how much it would cost them to eat.

"Maybe we could smuggle some CDs into the country to help cover expenses?" Jorge said, jokingly, seated at the kitchen table.

She looked disapproving. "The *Swiss* police enforce the law," she said, providing emphasis to distinguish them from the Recife police. Nonetheless, by early the next week she had gotten information as to how much they *could* legally take into the country—and what from Brazil might be sold there at a healthy profit. This went into her calculations, bringing down the uncovered expenses a notch.

Finally, after about three weeks, she perfected her calculations. She had some trouble, then, deciding when they could go, what with leaving the business, her mother, the children. All this seemed a bit out of proportion to Jorge. He made several suggestions, all of which encountered difficulties. He knew enough not to push. He only mentioned once that perhaps she should make the reservations as early as possible to be sure there was space, but she waved that away saying that, of course, she *knew* that.

Day followed day, week followed week, and Jorge heard no more. They were busy as usual, of course, so he didn't think often about the trip. When he did, he wondered why she hadn't said anything. Perhaps she had made the reservations and was waiting to tell him in her own time. If this had been a joint deal they were working on, he would have asked her. But this trip was Maria Amélia's dream. When she wanted to, she would let him know.

Shortly after midnight he woke up to find she was not in bed. Bleary eyed, he got up and wandered into their small living room. She was sitting on the sofa in her nightgown.

"Are you all right?" he asked. Normally she was a sound sleeper.

She looked up at him, her face wearing her worried look. Probably nobody but Jorge or her mother would have known it as her worried look—eyes focused, forehead concentrated—but that is what it was.

"I've been thinking," she said.

He plopped down on the sofa beside her and laid a hand on her knee.

"What about?"

She took a moment to collect her thoughts.

"It occurred to me there had to be a market for these things," she said. "So I looked around — talked to some people. I can sell it."

"Sell what?"

"The *trip*," she said, giving him a look that told him that should have been obvious.

"You want to sell the trip? The trip to Switzerland?"

She gave him another of those looks.

"I found a guy who's willing to buy it," she said. She named the price — it was substantial. "The Chevette's going to give out one of these days, we could use an extra room on the house, we always need money for the business… It doesn't make sense."

He thought for a moment, then shook his head.

"It doesn't make sense to *sell* the trip," he said.

"Of course it does," she answered. "We have needs, the money…"

He shook his head again.

"No ma'am," he said. "Some things aren't meant to be sold. We'll always have things we need, but this trip is your dream — it's a gift."

She still looked worried, so he used his best argument.

"You won it at the Sisters' bazaar," he said. "It's a gift from God."

In Jorge and Maria Amélia's world, God trumped money. Jorge looked at her, expecting to see relief on her face — permission to use this gift without thinking of the cost. But her face was still wrapped in worry.

The next day was Sunday. After mass they took the kids to the park for a while, then headed home for early afternoon dinner. About four o'clock, after resting, Jorge headed out to his work shed at the end of their small backyard. He had taken apart their broken toaster oven and was putting in a new piece when she came out carrying a glass of beer—a peace offering.

She skootched herself up and sat on his work table, watching him as he drank. He took a couple of sips and set down the glass.

"I've decided to sell the trip," she said.

He looked at her, pursed his lips, and shook his head.

"Why not?" she asked.

"Well, for one thing," he answered, "I don't want to spend the next forty years hearing how you had to sell your trip so that we could buy a new car, or add a room to the house, or whatever."

She looked at him with calculation in her eye. He had seen that look on her before, when she was negotiating and got boxed into a position from which there was no out, her last card played. Then her face relaxed and she sighed.

"I guess I'll have to tell you the truth," she said.

"I guess you will."

She sighed again. He waited.

"Ever since I was a little girl and first heard of Switzerland, I knew what it was like. Clean and cool and orderly. No litter, no garbage in the streets. Nobody poor. Polite people, honest people… everyone obeying the rules. Everything being done the way it *ought* to be done."

"Yeah. That sounds like Switzerland."

"That's what *we* think sounds like Switzerland," she said. "But is it really like that? I mean, there must be *some* litter on the streets, and some people who are rude. Some people who will cheat you, some things that are wrong."

"We'll find out when we go there," he said.

"I'm not sure I want to find out."

She lapsed into silence. He looked into her eyes—slightly above his own—and realized, as he sometimes did, that they were beautiful. Thoughts spun through his head.

"But suppose," he said quietly, "suppose it really is the way you think it is?"

She smiled at him and reached out to tousle his hair.

"Then," she said, "I probably wouldn't fit in."

They used the money—most of it—to build a bedroom for their son at the back of the house.

All of it, that is, except the money that went for the glass and frames. For three brand new posters of Switzerland—gladly given by Suttlier's—all of them clean and cool and speaking of peaceful order.

CARLA
(Rio de Janeiro, 1968 / Paris, 1973)

1

Carla Alves was twenty-three when she came from Rio de Janeiro to Paris: a woman of medium height, with dark blonde hair, a fresh white complexion, and thoughtful hazel eyes. At twenty-three she was an optimist by nature, raised in a home filled with love, and — despite all that had happened — tending deep inside to hope for the best, to trust people. But she was wary.

Unlike many Brazilians, she came to Paris not as an exile but as a graduate student. Her parents, both medical doctors, had married late — they were nearing their mid-thirties when Silvi, Carla's older sister, was born. Carla was born two years later. Both girls had been brought up to be well educated. To her parents' generation, being well educated included speaking French fluently.

Their parents showed no disappointment when neither daughter wished to enter medicine. Each girl, their mother said, had to find the discipline she liked best. In 1965, Silvi took the university entrance exams in sociology, placed among the highest students, and entered the Federal University. This was a year after the

Revolution that brought the military to power; student leaders had been arrested and the National Student Union had been closed down, but the heaviest crackdowns on the universities did not take place until 1969, and the climate when Silvi entered was tense but still fairly open. Within a few months, Silvi—with the intense intellectual passion that she brought to everything in life—was talking about slums, class structures, peasant leagues, and the need to change society. She became active in JUC—the Catholic university student league viewed by many as radical. Their parents, who were Catholic in a calm way, were bemused by this allegiance but probably, Carla thought when she looked back at that time, relieved that it was not a Marxist group. Her parents thought anything Silvi did was amusing but essentially wonderful. Carla herself smiled when she thought of Silvi in those days— her thin face, sparkling dark eyes, definite nose—waxing passionate about sociological theories that had seemed dry to Carla.

She had never been intellectual like Silvi. Silvi was brilliant, Carla was smart. She recognized this and in no way resented it. She loved and admired her sister with all her heart and it seemed only natural to Carla that Silvi was, in many ways, the center of family interest. Whatever Silvi said or did was interesting, compelling—in many ways, family life seemed to focus around her.

When Carla's own time came to take the university entrance exams, she took them in *belles-lettres*, a noncompetitive area in which she placed very well. She was accepted into the Federal University—which was free—but decided to go to the Catholic university because she had met and liked one of the professors there—an older woman who seemed kind and understanding. This decision was unusual as the Federal University, in addition to costing nothing, was considered more prestigious. But her parents cared little about prestige and did not have to be concerned about cost.

Like many middle-class Brazilians, their parents were not against the military takeover. Since the days of the monarchy, the military had been viewed by most Brazilians as the final political arbiter: if things got out of hand, the military stepped in, set them straight, then stepped out again. This had happened in 1945 and again in 1954. The Goulart government, which the military ousted in 1964, was not popular. But it had not occurred to Carla's parents—or anyone else of their class—that this time the military intended to stay, or that the takeover might touch them personally.

But that was before it happened.

It was in 1968.

Before the military takeover in 1964, students had been a highly vocal and visible force on the left. The repression following the military coup—the closing of the National Students' Union, the arrest and torture of many student leaders—and continued police surveillance pushed many of the radical groups underground. A tremendous, repressed tension permeated the university campuses.

In March, 1968, the tension burst in Rio. Student protests erupted over rising university fees, inadequate facilities, cuts in the national budget for higher education.

Carla went to a few protests because Silvi was helping to organize them, but she did not find them very interesting. Deep down inside, she agreed with Silvi's politics—it was obvious that things were unjust, that the poor and working people needed more to live on, needed to be treated more fairly. But she didn't like the protests—the shouting, the confusion—and didn't really see how they helped. It seemed to her that the students focused on things—like fees and budgets—that were peripheral at best. Her father always said that, in a country where half the population was illiterate, where public elementary schools were a joke, free federal universities only benefited the wealthy. But Silvi explained to her that the reasons for protests weren't really that important. They were leverage points, Silvi said, and Carla assumed she was right—Silvi usually was right. Even so, Carla found she couldn't get involved in the protests, and she usually stayed away from them.

She worried about Silvi, though. Late in March, the military police fired on student demonstrators and a student was killed. Carla came home late that afternoon and found her father and Silvi in the only shouting argument she had ever heard at home. Silvi didn't know what she was up against—her father's loud voice came rolling out of the living room—police, death squads: killers, torturers, filled with twisted hate against people like her—and Silvi's sharp reply: "Nothing will change if we *all* huddle in our houses like cowards." Her father's face red with anger as Carla entered the room, Silvi turning and walking out.

The next day, the funeral procession for the martyred student, marching along the Avenida Rio Branco in downtown Rio, was joined by thousands of people. Silvi was part of the committee that organized the procession. Carla didn't go, but she did go a week later to the student's seventh day mass, held in the Candelária Church on the Avenida Presidente Vargas. It was noon, and the huge, beautiful, baroque church was filled with mourners—students, politicians, people from nearby offices on their lunch break—expressing solidarity against the government. They came by the thousands, filling the church, blocking the entrances, filling the street outside and slowing traffic.

After mass, as Silvi and Carla were coming out of the church accompanied by a young priest from their parish, they became aware of a sudden silence, followed by a burst of confusion in front of them. Down the street, a line of mounted cavalry stretched across the avenue. As Carla watched, the soldiers drew their swords and started toward the crowd, bearing down, swords swinging. The crowd paused, hesitated, then broke, people running in panic back toward the church, off into side streets and buildings, the line of soldiers coming on. They seemed to be using the flat sides of their swords, but Carla saw a gash open on one man's neck as he ran, blood flowing profusely.

"*Damn* them!" she heard Silvi mutter, then saw her sister pushing forward, chin out, ready to personally confront the soldiers. Carla reached out and grabbed her arm; the priest caught hold of Silvi's other arm and together they pulled her back into the church. "They can't do that," Silvi said, turning to the priest, her dark eyes welling up with unshed tears at the injustice of it. "They are doing it," the priest said calmly, "stay here," and he stepped back out through the open door of the church onto the street. Carla pulled on Silvi's arm, but she wasn't strong enough to stop her, so she went out—reluctantly—with her. But by that time the cavalry had turned around, sheathed their swords, and were riding off, leaving a lot of people scared and a few bleeding, none seriously wounded or dead.

A few evenings later, Silvi didn't come home.

With all her activity, Silvi never stayed out late without letting them know. Her parents began telephoning some of Silvi's friends.

There had been, they learned, a quiet local crackdown on some of the university groups. Leaders of radical groups had been taken away—arrested, some people said. Others didn't say it to them, but the underlying fear came through—disappeared, dead.

For three days Carla and her parents barely slept, telephoning everyone they knew, her father and uncles going out, combing the jails, making contacts. On the third day they received a phone call and Carla's father rushed out of the house. "Silvi's alive," Carla's mother said to her, "you can go get some sleep," but neither of them slept until her father and uncle got home six hours later, bringing Silvi with them.

She was alive, but barely so. Not that her body was dead—it was bruised and beaten and God knows what else—but it was functioning. Her mind too was there, but her mind—which had been so brave and confident—stared out at Carla through terrified eyes in a pale face tensed with anxiety. Carla's mother took Silvi in her arms and cried, and after a while it seemed that Silvi cried too, tears running out of her eyes in an otherwise still face, as though the prisoner inside wanted to come out.

Her parents were medical doctors and that—God knows—at the moment was no blessing. Carla still remembered vividly her mother's face after she came out of Silvi's bedroom that first evening. It was a face filled with horror—a horror which her mother was not able to share with her until years later—and even then, only partly. Everything evil and despicable that could have been done to Silvi had been done.

Over the weeks, with love and patience, Silvi began to get better. Carla wanted to quit school and stay with her, but her parents wouldn't hear of it. Her mother suspended all her medical work to stay home with Silvi, and her father cut back a good deal on his. But Carla, they insisted, was young—she had to go on with life, look forward.

Still, Carla spent a lot of time with Silvi, coming home right after classes, allowing her mother to get out. She would sit with Silvi for hours—sometimes Silvi would listen to recordings of chamber music—the louder symphonic works made her nervous—or would let Carla read her stories. Carla had moved her bed into Silvi's room, which they now shared at night—the light always on. Sometimes Silvi would talk at night—never about what had happened to her—but usually she was quiet, removed into another world. She would scream out in her sleep, sometimes, waking up, and Carla would go over to her bed and hold her, glad for the times Silvi was able to cry. "Don't let the police take me," Silvi cried one night, fighting her way out of a nightmare with Carla hugging her. "We won't, *querida*, we won't," Carla answered. But she hadn't really understood, not really.

They never knew how she got the cyanide. She seldom went out of the house, never alone. She'd had visits from some of her student colleagues—a few had disappeared, but many had never even been arrested. In a house with two doctors, there were always odd bits of medicine around; for years Carla saw her parents torture themselves with questions as to whether they had left something lying about.

But Carla didn't think it made much difference. She had read about alcoholics—how they can be geniuses at obtaining liquor, outwitting everyone around them. She suspected that Silvi's mind was the same—focusing its vast intelligence on obtaining something Silvi needed to feel safe.

It happened one afternoon when Carla was coming home from the university. It was a beautiful, slightly cool day. She got off the bus and was walking down their quiet street when she heard the siren behind her. All her life she had heard sirens with their up-and-down wail—"hee-haw, hee-haw, hee-haw"—they had mocked the sirens when they were kids. But in the last few months, sirens sent shivers of horror down her spine.

The police car passed her and went on down the street. It stopped in front of her house a block-and-a-half ahead and Carla stood, paralyzed for a moment, then started to run. She reached the house out of breath and looked up. A man in uniform was coming down the front steps. "Wrong house," he said, smiling at her, and started toward the house next door. Carla slumped down in relief on the front step. She started to laugh, and suddenly she heard her mother screaming.

She ran through the front door and up the stairway to Silvi's room. Her mother and the maid were standing there, her mother weeping. Silvi was lying dead on the floor.

2

It was a few days after her twenty-fourth birthday. Carla had been in Paris for five months and, despite the many Brazilians there and her own fluent French, she was intensely lonely. It was the first time she had lived away from home, and she missed her parents—her mother's sensitive, intelligent groping to make sense of things, her father's wry humor and sharp, analytical mind, increasingly bitter, but trying to bring reason into the world. The closeness and memories that bonded the three of them, especially the last few years.

She passed through all the stages of being in a foreign land: the intense excitement of the first few days—the summer warmth of the city in late August, the shining rainy streets of September, the awareness of men's eyes following her as she passed the outdoor cafés—the feeling of being slightly exotic, graceful and pretty as any French woman yet in a slightly more fluid, more tropical way. Then the weeks of culture shock—deep longing for Brazil, for the warmth and casualness of her own people—fed up with anything French, their silly snobberies and fetishes—and especially the way the men looked at you—not the complementary way Brazilian men did, but in their apprising French way. Then again beyond into a deep appreciation of it all, a mixed love of Paris and a yearning for Rio de Janeiro, enjoying the rhythms of French life while echoing in one's head the counter-rhythms of home, being each day more fluent in the culture around her, growing more French while realizing more fully how deeply Brazilian she was.

But lonely. Light friendships with Brazilian students—some of them wanting to be only with other Brazilians, some of them wanting nothing to do with other Brazilians. Cordial relations with French students—a few of whom actually complimented her on her French. Good work in her classes, which she liked. A young black woman from Mozambique, with whom she enjoyed having coffee, listening to her strangely intoned Portuguese, laughing about the slang words of their different countries.

There had been men interested in her—a couple of the Brazilian students, a French boy (he really seemed boyish), a young assistant professor. But no one interesting enough to let her guard down, to let into her own world.

She came to the party because the girls in the house where she lived urged her to come. It was a mixture of people—the hostess was French, but most of the guests were Brazilian exiles. Someone had said that Miguel Arraes, the exiled populist governor of Pernambuco might be there, but he wasn't. There were a lot of well-known people, though—not people she knew, but one of her friends pointed them out to her: professors from Brasília and São Paulo, a couple of writers, a priest, an artist, a singer whose records she had listened to when she was a teenager. She thought that she should be impressed, but she wasn't. She felt detached and a bit bored. She slipped away from the group she had been talking to and wandered into another room.

And there he was. He was seated in a straight chair with its back pushed up against the wall, his head turned slightly away as though he were looking through the people in the crowded room and focusing on the large front window. He was of medium height, wiry thin, balding a little at the back—he was thirty-seven then, she found out later, but he looked older. He was intense, nervous, his skin pale, his nose like a sharp, hooked beak. He was not at all handsome. But he was so vulnerable—vulnerable and scared and needy—like Silvi in those last days—and Carla felt her heart splitting and opening as she walked over to him.

He turned and looked up at her as she approached his chair, and she smiled and said simply, "I'm Carla Alves," holding out her hand. He took her hand in his, half rising, holding his weight with his left arm against the back of the chair. "Jaime," he said, with the Brazilian way of using just his first name. He looked around for another chair, found one, and brought it over for her. They sat and talked. Mostly he talked and she listened.

"I looked over and saw him talking to you," Rogério, Jaime's closest friend in Paris, told her months later. "I didn't believe it. I hadn't seen Jaime talk that way in years—just talk and talk quietly to someone for hours."

It was from Rogério that she learned some of Jaime's

history—his work as a student activist in Pernambuco, his arrest and torture, his reputation as an economics professor—filling in the gaps, building a framework to explain things Jaime told her. Rogério and Jaime had grown up together in Recife, had attended the same private school, the same university. Rogério was a homosexual and had a sensitive, almost feminine understanding of Jaime. Once, when she had known him a few weeks, she asked him outright.

"Is Jaime gay?"

Rogério shook his head. "Oh, no," he said. "Jaime's just sort of asexual."

Which, Carla learned, was not quite true.

She sensed the distance in Jaime, of course. That was why she had asked. Unlike most men—especially Brazilians—Jaime did not seem to be concerned with her as a woman—at least not in a sexual sense. She knew that he was drawn to her, that he would talk to her as to nobody else—and she knew that if she were not a woman he would not be drawn in this way. If she took his hand he would hold hers, if she put her arm around his waist or kissed his cheek, she sensed he liked it. But he did not make any motion toward her, did not try to touch or kiss her.

One night he was at her apartment. She was sitting on the couch and he was lying with his head on her lap. They had been talking, but now were silent, and she was gently stroking his hair.

"They kept me in solitary confinement for six months," he said suddenly.

He had never talked about the time he was in prison. He had talked about his life as a child, his family, the days he spent working with Peasant Leagues in the sugar cane fields. He had mentioned his years at the university, his political activism, but distantly, as though it had all happened to another person at another time. He had shared his feelings about Paris, his life there, his teaching at the university, his book. Professorial, he had gone on at length about economics and how important it was to people—especially the poor; "Economics was made to serve mankind," he would say, paraphrasing the Bible, "not mankind to serve economics." It was a tribute to his talent for teaching that she was never bored by this, that he led her step by step through his thinking, making it alive, so that she saw an economic world peopled with real laborers and doctors and peasants.

But he spoke of prison only in passing: "Before I was arrested," "When I got out."

And then, tonight, starting with the six months in solitary, it came out, in bursts and jabs as he lay there with his eyes closed, her hand lying lightly on his head, and she listened, though she didn't want to listen, to the horrors. They came out all confused and jumbled because that time for him was—would always be— jumbled like sharp, cutting knives of nightmare. She held herself back from hushing him or from telling him that everything would be all right—could anything ever be all right again?—and listened, murmuring a word once in awhile to let him know she was listening. She listened because if he needed to tell her these things she needed to hear them, and, as tears began to glisten beneath his closed eyelids, tears began to stream from her own eyes so that, when he had finished and was sobbing in her arms, she was sobbing too and holding him close. And she thought, this is what they mean when they say a man and a woman become one.

A Note from the Author

Several readers have provided invaluable feedback on these stories. In addition to my wife Brenda King-Powers, I especially wish to thank my sisters Jean Todd and Eileen Buchanan, Jim and Haydée Ferreira McCarville, Richard Collins Davis, Gilberto Sodré de Carvalho, and Bernardo Aparício.

I also wish to remember my younger sister, Anita Powers Prouty (1949-2013), who died as this book was going to press. She loved stories, and would have loved to hold this book in her hands. As she blessed our lives with joy, may she continue to bless us with her memory and prayers.

ARTHUR POWERS went to Brazil in 1969 as a Peace Corps Volunteer and spent most of his adult life in that country. In the late 1970s, while practicing international law, he accompanied his wife in her work as a community organizer in the Rio de Janeiro slums. From 1985 to 1992, they worked for the Catholic Church in the eastern Amazon region of Brazil, organizing subsistence farmers and rural workers' unions in a region of violent land conflicts. Subsequently they directed relief and development programs in the drought-ridden Brazilian Northeast.

Arthur has received a Fellowship in Fiction from the Massachusetts Artists Foundation, three annual awards for short fiction from the Catholic Press Association, earned 2nd Place in the 2008 Tom Howard Fiction Contest, and 1st Place in the 2012 Tuscany Press Novella Award. He was a Press 53 Open Awards Finalist in 2011 and 2012. His poetry and fiction have appeared in numerous magazines and reviews. His award-winning novella, *The Book of Jotham*, is forthcoming from Tuscany Press in 2013.

Cover photographer AUGUSTO FROEHLICH says, "I do not usually follow my own dreams when working, but those of my clients. I am a photographer, just that, living in São Paulo, Brazil. As a friend said, I photograph life, including human life, natural world and human settlements, from caves to modern architecture."

As for the cover, Augusto adds, "The photo was taken while climbing our *Pico do Frade* (Peak of the Friar), which is a relatively low peak of about 1560m high (5118 feet). It is located in the state of Rio de Janeiro, almost on the border of the state of São Paulo. My wife and I went there, along with friends, guided by our friends at MW Trekking. What makes this photograph interesting is the beautiful granite wall, much higher than the mountains around it, and its closeness to the shore (6 km or 3.73 miles). These aspects give it an imposing presence. It is not very difficult to climb, but it is not accessible to the general public. The trails to the base are also a bit hard. I took this photograph about two hours before sunset."

Augusto has published two books of photography. The first, *Luz Marginal Procura Corpo Vago*, which he says translates to "Stray light searches for a [vague/available/vacant] body." It includes photographs by nineteen people from a course and workshop held by Brazilian photographer Gal Oppido and was created by the whole group, including Gal Oppido. The second book was a private project for a client that told the story of a small farm and depicts all aspects of farm life, ranging from homestead and historic places to crops and natural environment.

Augusto's website is www.froehlich-photo.com.

www.ingramcontent.com/pod-product-compliance
Lightning Source LLC
Chambersburg PA
CBHW031235260626
47169CB00007B/2307